MIXTAPE FOR

THE

APOCALYPSE

Jemiah Jefferson

"All in My Mind", "The Disease", "The Back of Love", "Rescue", "Stars Are Stars", "Over the Wall", "The Yo-Yo Man", "Going Up", "Nocturnal Me", "Blue Blue Ocean", and "Ocean Rain" written by Sergeant/McCulloch/Pattinson/DeFreitas. Published by Zoo Music/Warner Bros. Music Ltd.

"Song to the Siren" written by Tim Buckley and Larry Beckett. Published by Tim Buckley Music.

"How Soon is Now?" and "There Is a Light That Never Goes Out" written by Morrissey and Johnny Marr. Published by Universal Polygram International Publishing, Inc.

"Sound of Thunder" written by Duran Duran. Published by Gloucester Place Music, Ltd.

"The End" written by the Doors. Published by Doors Music Company.

Cover art by Ben Bittner

ISBN 978-1466310353

First printing September 2011

10 9 8 7 6 5 4 3 2 1

Printed in the United States of America

PROLOGUE

September, 1998
Bellingham, Washington

Autumn sunlight slants through the bookstore window and draws a perfect diagonal line in the air, an inverse of the letters I painted on the glass in shadows on the floor. I stop shelving for a while, wondering if I should grab my sketchbook and try to draw it. This moment is so rare, and any drawing done from memory can never be truly accurate. It could be days or weeks before the sun comes back out, or I might never see this particular angle and color of light again, and the opportunity to describe it gone forever.

I let it go. Let time pass. I shake my head, shrug it off, and return to stacking copy after copy of *Our Bodies, Ourselves*, the expanded new edition, now in oversized paperback. It'll sell like crazy to the new crop of college girls, the ones who saved themselves, or the ones who hadn't and wished they had. These budding feminists are our biggest customers. Mom thinks I should pick one out and go on a date with her, since I'm only a little bit older than most of them, but I don't feel quite right thinking about them in that way. I'm not quite there yet.

I'm not ready for a new girlfriend. I don't know if I'm over the old one yet.

"Squire," my mother says, snapping her fingers. "Hey, you, kid, with the face. Squire, honey, c'mon, wake up."

"Huh? What." I meet her eyes. She's behind the register counter, smirking at me over her glasses. "Sorry; I was thinking about, um, women," I murmur, turning back to the bookshelves.

"You can think and shelve at the same time. The syllabi get handed out tomorrow; we've got to get those books on the shelf before we open.

Anyway, you got mail, sweetie." She waves envelopes at me—white ones that are probably bills, and a fattish padded manila envelope. There's also a magazine. Mom looks curiously at the cover. "*Fortean Times*? What's that about?"

"Supernatural phenomena," I say, taking the mail. "You know, like vampire cults, ESP, the chupacabra."

"Never heard of it."

"It's British. It's pretty tongue-in-cheek, but kind of scholarly."

"Did Larry put you up to this?"

"No." I smile at her. "I ordered it myself. I used to pick it up off the newsstand. Y'know, before."

She kisses me on the cheek, a simple warm peck; perfect. She gives fantastic mom kisses. Mom doesn't ever ask me about Before; I don't know if it's too upsetting, or if it just doesn't make any sense. I can understand that perspective. She's done a good job of pretending not to worry that I'm going to flip out again, but my therapist's emergency number is still taped to every single phone in the building. I'd like to reassure her that I'm fine, but she's going to believe what she wants to believe.

She tosses her gray-stranded braid over her shoulder and replies breezily, "Oh, okay. That's fine with me. Besides, it's out of our 'market niche.'" She makes pantomime quote marks in the air. "The local weirdos can get their vampire cult stories at the other bookstores."

I play along. "I'm glad I qualify as a local weirdo."

"The very best there is. You know what; why don't you take off for the rest of the day? Tomorrow we're going to have a stampede. You should take it easy while you can. I'll finish up over there." She gives me a smile that's only slightly sad. "Go get a cup of coffee—on second thought, go upstairs and make a nice cup of hot Ovaltine."

"Oh, great; powdered drink instead of an afternoon's pay. I'm going on strike."

"Hot Ovaltine kicks ass. Full o' minerals." She gives me a quick hug, and picks up where I left off with the shelving. "Go look at your mail. The sun's out. Maybe do some art."

Upstairs in the apartment I wash my hands and put the kettle on. I open the curtains and sit at the kitchen table, parking myself exactly in the center of the square of sunlight.

Naturally, I open the big envelope first, pulling out a slim hardbound book with a folded piece of paper rubber-banded to it. The paper is stationery from the Wellington Bed and Breakfast, Perth, Australia, its top edge raggedly torn from a notepad. I don't know anybody in Australia, but I recognize that handwriting.

> *August 27, 1998*
>
> *Yo yo Squire,*
>
> *How are you? I miss the hell out of you! I'm sorry I haven't written you before now. Or called you. Or . . . anything. I guess I was scared. Or angry, or probably a lot of stuff mixed together that I couldn't untangle. I needed some distance before I wanted to make contact with you again, but I always knew I would. I'm not mad anymore. I know you couldn't help it, and even the parts that you could help, I don't mind anymore. I still want to be friends and I think we can be; I hope you think so too.*
>
> *Australia is fun, but I miss Portland. I'm having a good time hanging out with my dad, though. He is shooting footage for his next documentary project. I can't believe it! I'm a production assistant! I get paid and I'll be in the credits and everything. It is so not glamorous, though. Who knew those photocopying skills eventually come in handy.*
>
> *I actually ran into Kimmie and Renton Sutton and they told me you were friends with their dad. They are really cool—I met them in a pub a couple of nights ago and we've been hanging out a lot. They made me think about you. I didn't tell them too many details about you, just that we used to live together in Portland before I came out here, and that you live in Bellingham with your mom now. Their dad sounds pretty amazing, which would make you being friends with him make a lot of sense. I think you should totally write a comic about him. Just think about it! No pressure!*
>
> *I'm sending you one of your journals. I found it when I was packing my stuff for shipping while you were in the hospital. I didn't read it, I promise. I thought that you might like to have this so you know that it's safe. You can burn it or whatever, but at least you know where it is.*
>
> *I miss you a lot—so much—I wish you were here—but hopefully I'll see you again before too long. Give your Mom a kiss for me.*
>
> *love (still),*
>
> *Lise*

I laugh. "I'm not mad anymore, either," I say out loud.

Then I feel guilty, and sorry for Lise. She must think that just having access to my journals, where I wrote down all of the crazy things that I couldn't say, is going to send me over the edge. Like Mom, I guess she doesn't understand that it's not like that. And I was so shitty to her when I was in the middle of it. But I'm better now. I changed. My thoughts changed. Stabilized. I survived. The world didn't end.

The journals didn't make me insane; that happened on its own. I only wrote down what I thought. Personally, I think it helped me. I can't even consider what I would have been like if I hadn't written them.

I feel a sense of relief having this missing piece of myself. I've had all of the journals from my time of mental distortion, except for this one, the last one that I did Before. It's not even completely filled, with a handful of blank pages at the end.

Ever since I moved back up here with Mom, I've been itching to read the journals that I wrote in the time Before. Without euphemism, it was just last year, but I have huge gaps in my memory from that time. I remember a lot of it, but not enough; I want details. I want them back.

I want them even though I know they're grim and terrible details that lost me my previous life almost as effectively as if the world had ended, and I'm currently in some kind of afterlife. But Lise's package anchors me. It was real, and it happened, and she remembers it, too. She was there.

I take the journal and letter into my bedroom, and press Play on the face of my battered portable stereo. A Björk song resumes in the middle of its orchestral introduction. I didn't think I liked Björk until Shandy succeeded in changing my mind.

Well, it's still the same mind. It's just missing a few pieces from the center of the puzzle.

I slide my foot locker from under the bed and open it, briefly imagining that it's the Ark of the Covenant and its contents could melt my face off, but instead of the flesh-dissolving wrath of an Abrahamic god, it's only full of journals and sketchbooks. Once I find the first in the series of notebooks inside, I rest it face-up on the floor, lie on my bed, and examine it from a safe distance. The first journal is housed in a grey composition book with a marble-printed cover, the black plastic spine now cracked; it makes a crunchy sound when it opens and closes. There is a faded Hitting Birth sticker on the cover, my name in black-marker block capitals written on the inside cover.

As much as I try to deny the power that a simple object has over me, I still feel an almost supernatural jolt of emotional power just from seeing what my handwriting looked like. It's so precise, like I knew exactly what I was talking about.

ONE: On Any Other Day, That Might Seem Strange.

7 August 1997, 4:07 p.m.
You say stop looking for answers
and reasons they're all in your mind

Ah, that's better—nothing like a good quote to overcome the terrifying *tabula rasa* of the first blank page in a blank book. That one, of course, is Echo and the Bunnymen. They are one of the things that defines me, Michael Bronwynn Squire, just like it says on the tin.

This is a journal. I'm documenting. If you are not me, please do me a heap big favor and PUT MY MOTHERFUCKING BOOK DOWN YOU PIG-SHIT EATING COCKSUCKER!!!! Still reading? You must be me, then. Hi!

I'm supposed to be at work right now, but I called in sick, claiming a migraine (a very convenient excuse. How can they prove me wrong? A CAT scan?). Instead of going to Link-Up and instructing a whole new wave of subhumans on how to merge onto the Information Superhighway, so that they too can "surf" the "web," I did something good. I went to Art Store. I love Art Store—I love anything called only what it is—Liquor Store, Restaurant, Café. I bought a package of watercolor paper, a set of Micron pens, more crow quill tips, and a huge, lovely bottle of dark green ink that I actually kissed as I was in the checkout line. The cute underage goth girl who works there laughed at me. I don't know her name, but she knows mine—I'm in there about once a week, usually when I know she's working. She was wearing some kind of tattery velvet thing today—hair up in chopsticks.

Also I bought this composition book to use as a journal. I've been using my sketchbook too much for random text observations, and not enough for drawing street corners, hands, or ugly people on the bus. Lise suggested I start writing a diary, so here we are. Actually, both Lise and my mother have been on me to start a diary; Mom because she thinks it'll improve my writing skills (she'd rather have an author for a son than a lowly comics artist), and Lise, so that I'll stop talking about myself so much. I think I can quote her—"Obviously you're a supreme egotist, Squire. There's nothing inherently wrong with that—but sometimes I don't want to hear about what your favorite kinds of cheese are, and a detailed explanation why."

Lise is my best friend. Mom runs a bookstore in Bellingham. They are best friends, too. I have to co-best-friend Lise. She and my mom have been friends for one day less than Lise and I have been friends. I try not to be jealous, but I kind of am. I'd kind of like to have Lise all to myself, and also I know that the two of them must talk about me. But it is what it is.

Right now, this minute, just past four on a hot afternoon, I'm sitting in my room having some coffee, writing at my desk, and listening to a mix tape Lise made for me. Side two starts with "Temple of Dreams" by Messiah. Only two years after it was released, it already sounds quaint. I remember when I thought this 160-beats-per-minute shit was the hardest of the hard, and now it sounds like Lawrence Welk. Techno hit the wall after 180; once you can't dance to it anymore, it gets too avant-garde for the Youth Majority.

My housemates Melissa and Rob are in her room, listening to the Beach Boys. Half the reason why I put on Messiah is because I know that techno annoys Melissa. She's one of those people who's a fascist about music made after 1968. I like old stuff as much as the next fellow, but for God's sake, join the twentieth century sometime.

Things I need to do today:
-Balance checkbook. Yuck.
-Return videos (BEFORE 6 p.m.!)
-Check e-mail. Yeah, yeah, yeah.

-Check in at Squirrell and see if Lucas is done penciling page 17.

-Call Mom.

-Call Lise.

Old-fangled or not, I love this track, overused Funky Drummer beat and all. *Did I dream you dreamed about me? It's time to start RUNNING!*

After finishing that first entry, I'd closed the book with a resounding slam and went back to the kitchen to rinse my coffee mug. My housemate Melissa and her boyfriend Rob were in the kitchen, cooking another one of their fright-meals that always seemed to contain lima beans or TVP, and from which Melissa never ate more than a few bites, leaving the remainder in the fridge for me to discover and toss weeks later. I leaned against the doorjamb of the kitchen and lit a cigarette, trying to think of a devastatingly witty and cutting remark. Unfortunately, before I could come up with it, the telephone rang. Melissa and Rob completely ignored it, so I had to run across the room and pick it up. "Laika, Melissa, and Squire's Angst Volume Warehouse, how can I take your order?" I answered.

"Hi, honey."

I sighed. "Oh, hi, Mom."

"You sound even more bitter than usual."

I walked the phone on its long cord back into my room and shut the door. "Oh, it's that fucker Rob. You know, Melissa's boyfriend? I'm so sick of him being in my house smelling like Brut and scratching his basket all day. He doesn't pay rent; he doesn't pay bills; he just sits around the house and stinks."

As usual, Mom laughed her ass off at my ranting. "Why don't you just confront him, Squire? It's your house, too."

"Confront? Me? You mean the kid who saw the bowl of every toilet in high school from close up, courtesy of the wrestling team? That's a great one, Mom. Why don't I just join the Green Berets?"

"Come on. Get Laika to help you."

"No. Laika doesn't care about him one way or the other—she's never home. She's over at her girlfriend's house all night. Rob's a really scary guy. Lise saw him beat up some guy last weekend. We're talking bloody nose here. And it wasn't even for any reason—he was just drunk."

"And you told me you wanted to live with these people. What happened to 'Melissa is such an awesome girl, Mom, you're gonna love her,' huh? I told you, Squire; never move in with friends. Especially friends from your college days."

"Yeah, I know. It's everybody's favorite phrase, 'I Told You So.'" I leaned against my art table, scattering pencils and wads of Art Gum. Melissa and Laika and I had been Student Center fixtures all throughout senior year, holding down couches, drinking hot tea, smoking, and filling out crossword puzzles. While we each had our own distinct social group—me with the artists (and Lise, who wasn't in school but hung around with us on campus), Laika with the stoners, and Melissa with the hippies—the three of us spent hours a day with one another, courteously bringing each other tea and newspapers and keeping an ear out for good drug deals. "I thought I could trust them. We all knew each other so well. But she just turned on me all of a sudden. I think it was Rob. Everybody likes Rob except me and Lise. Nobody can understand why I don't love living with the big lug."

"Speaking of Lise, tell her to call me. I haven't heard from her in weeks!"

"She said she sent you e-mail. She's actually been wondering why you haven't replied."

"Oh, actually, that's what I was calling you about. I can't get the internet to work."

I ground my teeth. "Mom, it's totally easy; I even wrote you custom instructions."

"Squire, you're assuming a level of fundamental knowledge that I just don't have. Pretend you're teaching a six-year-old how to do it."

"Half the six-year-olds in America could teach me my job."

My mother engaged in a whining contest with me, and as usual, she won. Her adulthood was already firmly established, so much easier to set aside when the need arose. "Bronwynn, sweetie, c'mon, help out your old stupid mother; it'll only take a minute."

While I walked my mother though the software installation and set-up process, Melissa and Rob got into a shouting match right outside my door, shattering my concentration and making a delicate explanation impossible. Mom announced with a sort of gleeful disappointment, "It looks like I've had a system crash; what should I do now?" At roughly the same time she said "crash," I heard glass break outside. "Hang on, Mom," I bit out, threw the phone receiver down as hard as I could onto the floor, and stormed outside. Someone had thrown an empty jelly jar against my door and it lay in shattered pieces right in my path.

"WILL YOU SHUT THE FUCK UP!" I bellowed.

The next thing I knew I was slumped against the wall with a spreading blossom of pain coming from my chest. It took about three tries before I could breathe successfully. Rob stood over me, shaking his canned-ham-sized fist. "Don't talk to my girlfriend like that!" he yelled back.

"...What .. ?" I said.

Melissa was in the far corner of the room, shaking her head sadly at me, like I'd pulled a Jerry Lewis and tripped over the low brown pile. "Get up, Squire. God, you're so lame. This has nothing to do with you."

"I'm . . ." To my horror, I felt tears starting up in my eyes. "I'm trying to talk to my mother on the phone . . ."

"Just stay out of our business, Squire. And clean up that glass before somebody gets cut." Melissa and Rob turned as one, and disappeared into her room.

My body felt like one big bruise. I'm not much more substantial than tissue paper at the best of times. I dragged myself back into my room and put the phone receiver back together. "What took you so long?" Mom's voice came to me as if through a wind tunnel. "This is long distance . . . and I'm not made out of money, which you know . . ."

"Rob hit me," I muttered. "Really hard. In the sternum."

"Oh, Squire. What did you say to him?"

"To *him*? What did I say to *him*?" I laughed. "He's a fuckin' asshole, Mom. He just hit me for no reason."

"Squire, I think you should move out."

"Mom . . . Could we . . . could we try this again later? Why don't you just call your ISP? At least that's a local call."

"Well, okay. But I think you should stand up to this guy before you get really hurt."

"Too late," I said, and hung up.

Later that night I hung out with Laika in her room. She had a TV and a very nice two-chambered bong, and she was always packing, thanks to her hippie girlfriend. We watched sci-fi and ate cookies. "Fuckin' Rob," I mumbled after a couple of pleasant silent hours.

"Do you have a bruise?" Laika asked.

I looked down my T-shirt. "No," I said with disappointment.

"He's totally never been mean to me," said Laika distantly. "I don't know . . . you guys just don't get along."

"No shit. I should move out."

"You haven't paid this month's rent yet," Laika reminded me.

"Yeah, I forgot."

"Bullshit, you forgot."

"I forgot," I insisted.

"You should cough it up," said Laika knowingly. "You're more than a week late. That's not cool. And stop listening to that stupid eighties music."

"It's not stupid," I protested, but I smiled. "I like it. It's important to me. I wouldn't tell you to stop listening to the fucking Gipsy Kings."

"Screw you." Laika leaned over me to grab another cookie. "My girlfriend is moving to Seattle," she said.

"That sucks," I replied. "Why?"

"She hates Portland." Laika shrugged. Her reddish blonde hair was parted in the middle and never particularly combed; it just hung greasily onto her shoulders. On her, it was actually appealing. She was a kind of a beautiful grunge waif who genuinely didn't care about her looks, but was attractive nonetheless, even if I'd never personally been attracted to her. We were buddies, having met when we were both trying to hit on the same girl. (Laika got her.) "I can see her point. There's nothing to do here."

"There's plenty to do," I protested.

"Like what? Go play video games for a nickel? See some overpriced movie, drink some overhyped beer? Oh boy, the Rose Garden. Oh boy, the Blazers. Oh boy, Everclear. That's the problem with this town—all its faults are the things that people love about it and the people . . . the people like . . . aw, fuck, you know what I'm talking about."

"No, actually, you're rambling. And I hate Everclear. I'm not asking Portland to marry me or anything; I just don't see what's so wrong with it."

Laika chuckled and wrinkled her freckled nose. "Anyway . . ."

"Was that the last cookie?"

"Uh, yeah. Sorry."

"You suck," I said affectionately. "Thanks for the smoke."

"Any time, pal, any time. You know that. We're still good." She shook my hand elaborately, her handful of silver rings digging gently into me. Her nails were very short, and when it occurred to me why she kept them that way, I took my hand back, turned away so she wouldn't see me, and sniffed it. It just smelled like marijuana, which made sense.

10 August, 12:35 p.m.

My favorite things (per request; Lise is sick of hearing about them).

-Kisses. As if I remember what they're like.

-Tim Roth, especially in *Reservoir Dogs*. His fake American accent reminds me of Uncle Bill.

-Rapidograph pens.

-My Internet flirt object, "Juba." She's fifteen and she and her friend "Arachne" take pictures of themselves wearing nothing but black lace underwear, their fragile wrists bound up with black duct tape, duct tape over their eyes, etc., and then they send me the pictures as e-mail attachments. I suppose I shouldn't encourage them, but she seems so innocent and fun and naughty, and Juba writes me all the time to complain about how close-minded high school is. I haven't seen nipple yet, but Juba promises me that it's forthcoming. They'll have to do it when Arachne's parents aren't home. They are fans of my comic book.

-Alex Toth. My favorite artist. Second is Aubrey Beardsley, though he never did comics. I'd like to bridge that gap.

-My bike. I don't ride it enough.

-Foccacia sandwiches at Cafe Triste.

-The word "pugnacious."

-Getting off work and going drinking with Lise.

-Echo and the Bunnymen. Hands down my favorite group ever. Scratch that—my FAVOURITE band ever. I think they deserve the British U. I don't care that they broke up years ago; it's like being upset that James Dean is dead. It's just a beautiful shame, that's all.

-Beatnik goths. I consider myself one (perhaps wrongly, but who creates a valid cultural category, if not the man himself?). More beatnikky, actually. I even went so far as to grow a goatee, thinking it would help my weak chin, but so many people laughed at me—even random people on the street—that I shaved it off. That's one of my most painful memories.

-The word "slovenly."

6:00 p.m.

Back from my cigarette break. Only an hour to go. I don't know if I can even stand it. Link-Up's T1 went down at 2 and we've been apologizing and explaining our asses off all afternoon. I don't know why I went into tech support—I hate people and I don't want to help them. I don't want to explain it all and yet make it feel like I'm not patronizing them. Dammit, I *am* patronizing them. I had to learn all this shit from scratch, why can't they? I shouldn't complain, I guess—it does pay me pretty well for a whole shitload of slacking—but goddamn it, I hate people. Most of all I hate Trace. He's a fucker. I hate knowing he owns all of this. The sight of him makes my hackles rise and the amount of tension in the entire room increases a thousand fold. It's not just me. We spend a lot of time writing each other e-mail across the room, screaming in ASCII bitterness about Trace's injustices to both customers and employees. Or sometimes just how much we hate Trace's flat ass and his carefully combed thinning hair and his total lack of lips. And how we think he must jerk off in his office over the latest issue of *Wired*. That zinger was Thomas's, and was so brilliant that I saved the e-mail, a somewhat risky move. Trace thinks nothing of searching through our

personal accounts; he hands out the passwords, so he knows them all. We can't really hide from him, not on Link-Up's machines.

Oh, well. One more call and I'm going to bugger off.

Five minutes before seven, I turned my phone off and started gathering my things. Summoned by my body language, some of the usual crew wandered over, Randy and Dave specifically. "It's five minutes early," said Randy, crunching on curiously strong peppermints.

"So it is," I said.

"Don't let Trace catch you." Dave picked up from where Randy had left off. I had given up trying to guess which was trying to be more like the other; they had been friends so long that they were essentially the same mind controlling two separate bodies. They were quite different physically—Randy tall, sandy blond, piercingly emotionless eyes; and Dave short and dark with aviator glasses that were so flyspecked and smudgy that it made my head ache. I could never live with such filthy glasses. "Big Bossman's been on the warpath about people signing off early."

"Doesn't he have better things to do?" I grumbled, pulling my shoes back on.

Dave leaned way over me and squinted at my computer screen. "What's that?" he asked.

"What, my desktop? Oh; that." He pointed at the caricature of our company's president I'd done while on the phone earlier today, stuck onto the side of my monitor with a piece of tape. I'd drawn him as Dracula—long hollow cheeks, bristling eyebrows, huge maniacal eyes—in other words, a pretty good likeness. "I should take that down."

"No, no, man, leave it up. That's really good."

"I am an artist, you know," I said, standing up and flicking off my monitor. "Excuse me; gotta get." Before they could give me any more advice, I was out the door, in the elevator, and down on the street.

Lise worked at Pronto Printing, the copy shop downstairs and around the corner from Link-Up Telecommunications, Inc. The shop was a hive of activity that evening—yellow polo shirts darting back and forth, customers squirming in line, the constant soothing techno hum of high-powered copiers and the slap-slap-chunk-chunk of bound, stapled, and collated copies falling into bins. Lise, behind the counter, looked up from a stack of pinkish forms she was stuffing into manila envelopes. "Yo, yo," she said, smiling. "Gimme a minute."

"Walkin' the dog." I leaned against the counter to wait, fingering a cigarette in the most inviting way possible. Lise Severina Ballard is seventeen days older than me, one inch shorter, twenty pounds heavier (sometimes a little more), and has always had shorter hair than me. She has a heart-shaped face and brown eyes with silvery-grey around the pupils. At that point, we had known each other for nine years, since we were both fifteen. She'd gone to college in Olympia, and I'd gone to Portland. She'd dropped out after her second year and moved to Portland because she couldn't make enough "friendly connections" in Olympia. On that day, her hair was about an inch and a half long all over, growing out brown from a brassy yellow bleach job, heavily gelled so that the blond parts looked like porcupine quills. She's the only person I've ever known who can look good in a yellow Pronto Printing polo shirt.

After finishing the envelope stuffing, she disappeared into one of the back rooms and came out wearing half-shredded blue-jean cutoffs and a plain white T-shirt, hoisting her purse over her shoulder. Her breasts looked amazing, but I didn't mention it. Outside, she lit my cigarette and one of her own and we began walking slowly to the bus stop. "What's the matter with you, Squire?" she demanded after we'd gone a few blocks without speaking.

"What . . . ?"

"Usually, the minute you see me, you start talking non-stop. When you have something that's bugging you, you make me drag it out of you. So I'm dragging."

"Oh . . . work sucked particularly today. Oh, yeah, and Rob was such an asshole to me the other day."

"Melissa's boyfriend? The ogre?"

"More like a troll. They were having a little lover's quarrel right outside my room while I was trying on the phone with Mom trying to fix her modem, so I went out and told them to pipe the fuck down; and then the son of a bitch hit me in the chest so hard I couldn't breathe."

"What?" Lise laughed in disbelief.

"He—fuckin'—" I struggled to find the right words to describe my outrage. "He fuckin' hit me."

"What a dick!"

"And somebody threw a glass against my door, but they made me clean it up."

"That guy's a fuckin' psycho."

"He's gonna kill me in my sleep."

"Probably," Lise supplied helpfully. "Anyway, let's drink. I'll buy you one. Where ya wanna go?"

"Triste. I'm hungry."

"Triste?" she whined.

"What's the matter with Triste? It's our favorite café."

"It's *your* favorite café. Besides, we always go there. They don't even like you there. They don't even have *booze* there."

"We'll just look in. I'll grab a sandwich. Then we can go . . . I don't know, somewhere else."

"You're such a creature of habit."

"I'm hanging out with you, aren't I?" I pointed out.

We did some mock slap-fighting on the bus stop that continued on the bus. The other passengers stared at us. I got self-conscious and stopped, but Lise licked her finger and jammed it into my ear. "People are looking, Squire!" she screamed, laughing.

"Shut up!"

"Pee-ple are loo-king!"

"Shut! Up!" My face was on fire.

"You kids cut it out back there," came the bus driver's voice, authoritative and godlike through the P.A. Everyone else on the bus laughed nastily, and I sunk as far as physically possible into the millimeter of plush covering the seat.

Cafe Trieste was in its usual state on a Wednesday night, populated by about ten people sitting around sipping tall glasses of iced coffee, picking at massive sagging slabs of tiramisu, cheesecake, or their Legendary Scary Foccacia Monster sandwiches that always fell apart into your lap if you tried to be macho and pick them up like ordinary sandwiches. Lise knew that I wanted my usual, so she went up to the counter while I sat at a table along the wall and whipped out my diary.

7:31 p.m.

At Café Triste. Actually it's "Trieste" but it's such a sad and maudlin little place that my drunken mispronunciation suits it perfectly. It always smells like bleach, no matter how much Nag Champa they burn trying to cover it up. The general clientele is boring and pretentious, though the "café scene" that Triste was trying to join is kind of already dead, and the only reason why I come here really is because they put crack or something into their sandwiches—I'm hopelessly addicted to them.

The slutty chick isn't working tonight, it doesn't look like. Scheiss. I was maybe going to try to put the moves on her. On the other hand, I doubt I could have done it with Lise around, since she calls bullshit when she sees it. This chick—her name's Marcy, blech—is the kind of willowy femme that Lise loves to hate—she wears T-shirts made for four-year-old boys and miniskirts slit up to the ass. I saw her panties once—greyish, cotton. Not too exciting. Juba *et. al.* have spoiled me—I swear their lingerie budget must be something like the

Lise came back to our table with glasses of coffee. "What are you doing, Bronwynn?" she asked, ripping her straw paper with her teeth.

"Journal," I said, covering it with my elbow and finishing the last sentence.

gross national product.

"Really? No wonder you've been so quiet. You're not drawing in it, are you?" She grinned.

I arched one eyebrow. "Of course not, what do you take me for? Besides, I left my sketchbook at home. I'm not drawing right now. I have a new path." I put the cap back on my pen. "I'm a letterer."

"Bullshit, Squire. Look at you. Every inch the art fag. The unkempt hair; the Truman Capote glasses. A black T-shirt and black jeans in the summer! Everything about you says 'tortured fanboy'. . ."

Lise's soliloquy was interrupted by the less-than-cute waiter, the manager's boyfriend in fact, bringing my sandwich. He slopped it on the table, spattering me with drops of runny pesto. "Hi, Lise," he said, pointedly ignoring me. "How come you don't come in any more?"

"I do come in," she protested. "I come here with Squire every damn week."

I stuffed a corner of sandwich in my mouth and bent over the book again.

These Triste fuckers really annoy me sometimes. I think that dweeb—Charles or Chopper or something—knows that I've had a really shitty day. God, I hate my job. I hate Trace. The thought of him curdles my blood—the little psychological games he plays, the smiley sheen of sexism and sadism that he puts on, the little "deals" he cuts people. Moll told me that, before I was hired, Trace told Moll she could have a promotion if she would agree to "not make waves." She took it. Then he tried to ask her out. She refused, and she was instantly demoted back to the phone support department. I'm glad I'm not a nice-looking chick, that's all I have to say. I just hope that son of a bitch hasn't been reading my e-mail.

"Squire . . . that's really rude . . ."

"What?" I almost knocked my coffee glass over, I was so startled.

"I'm trying to talk to you," Lise said, smiling patiently. "Put it away."

I slid the notebook under the table. "Oh. What were you saying?"

She ran her hand over her porcupine quills. "I was telling you that I'm getting a raise at work, and they're thinking about making me primary shift manager on Tuesdays and Thursdays."

I blinked. "Oh? Yeah?" But Lise hated her job, too.

"I mean, I can do it; it's not like it's hard. I'm excited about the money, though. I've been working there for long enough, they might as well throw me a bone now."

"Oh, well I guess that's cool." I smiled and looked down into my lap, so it wouldn't seem like I was wildly jealous of her, and hating my own job more than ever.

"Fuck you, it's awesome," she laughed, reaching across the table to poke me in the chest. Right where Rob punched me.

"Ow," I said. I glared at her, indignantly arching one eyebrow.

She arched her eyebrow back at me. In high school we called this "a Spock-Off." "You deserved that. I know you hate me right now."

"I could never hate you," I said. "You just bought me a sandwich. In the ancient land of my people, that's basically love."

"Oh, wow, your people are from Moochistan, too? I miss the old country." She smiled at me, and I smiled back, and everything was good.

Later, we went back down the street to the Cazbar, and Lise and I drank several kamikazes apiece. She actually went down for the count—forehead pressed into her arm on the table, mumbling incoherently—and in the interval I wrote more. My handwriting is appallingly poor here.

At the Cazbarr w/Lise. I have had five cocktails and Lise has had four. They are hella strong. She is passing out. She didn't eat first. I am pretty good at holding my liquor, which is another thing that Triste sandwiches are good for. I love to get drunk in bars. That's what your twenties are all about—getting totally fucked up and learning why it's dumb, so you don't spend the rest of your life as a pathetic alkie. Like most of my British relatives. They've all got cirrhosis and cancer and whatever. They drink a ton every night. The older ones. I don't know many of my younger relatives, except for James, the one that's a little younger than me, who is a complete raver and never sleeps because he's rolling on Ecstasy all the time. He doesn't drink though. It's weird. I have never taken Ecstasy. I kinda want to.

A toast! To cannibal women!

Lise perked up eventually, and walked me to "the fork in the road," the intersection of the street she lived on, and the street I lived on. "Merry meet and merry part, and merry meet again," Lise slurred, waving at me. I stood still and watched her stagger backward a few steps, waving and throwing me kisses. Just in time she turned around, narrowly avoiding colliding with a utility pole.

I walked slowly back to my own house. It was a lovely night—warm and clear, all the stars pricked out in the sky like pinholes in a blue velvet backdrop. It seemed a waste to go inside and destroy this happy tipsy feeling, so I sat on the porch and smoked another cigarette before I went in.

The house was quiet and dark. I tiptoed in, shutting the door and locking it behind me as quietly as I could. Despite my best efforts, though, Rob shuffled down from Melissa's room as I was in the kitchen getting a glass of water. His eyes were completely closed and he felt his way along the kitchen cabinets. I stood stock still, not even breathing, hoping he'd just go past me to the bathroom and not notice that I was there, but he paused and cocked his head back, as if regarding me through his closed eyelids. His package hung distended and gruesomely large inside his permanently stained white underwear—I couldn't take my eyes away from it and I couldn't breathe.

"Izzat you, you little dipshit?" he muttered.

I said nothing. His eyeballs darted uneasily behind his closed lids. He was sleepwalking, it seemed, or trying to freak me out, one of the two. It was working, if the latter was his intention.

"I'm gonna kill you one of these days," Rob mumbled.

I drew in my breath before I could stop myself.

He paused, grunted, and added, "I'll kill you in your sleep."

I slid down the kitchen cabinets until I was sitting on the floor, then I crab-walked to the kitchen doorway. He lumbered forward after me like the living dead.

My foot tripped on the living room carpet, and I collapsed onto my butt. He stood over me, still mumbling something about killing under his breath. Melissa appeared at the kitchen doorway, dressed only in a tie-dyed T-shirt, her pubes a dark stain visible under the hem. She grabbed Rob by the arm and steered him back toward the kitchen. "He's sleepwalking again," she mumbled, yawning.

"He says he's going to kill me," I said faintly.

"He says that every night. Just go to bed."

"How long has he been sleepwalking?"

"Since he was a kid," Melissa explained. "It's stress-related."

"Oh," I said, and got up. "Stress-related, huh? What's he got to be stressed about?"

"You wouldn't understand," she said, glaring over her shoulder. "All you care about is yourself. Rent check by the time I leave for work tomorrow morning at eight. Remember to add fifty bucks for the late fee. Shithead." She guided Rob up the stairs and slammed the door behind her.

Once I was able to stand up, I got the rent check off my desk and set it in an obvious place on the kitchen counter. Afterward I lay on top my bed in my clothes and shoes. I wasn't exactly scared, but I was badly shaken. I spent the night staring at the luminous green numbers of the clock, listening to the infinitesimal click of the digital numbers reforming themselves, as if waiting for a bomb to go off. When the sky outside began to lighten, I took a cold shower, put on clean clothes, and left before the sun rose.

12 August 9:45 p.m.

Oh, shit, I forgot to write anything yesterday. I got up super early and went to Link-Up. Juba sent me some more pictures; fairly ordinary ones, nothing naked or kinky. Her at the mall, wearing a letterman's jacket and really tight black jeans. She's leaning over the railing as if to spit into a fountain. She wears a lot of mascara. I can probably make a good panel out of it if I figure out an approach; she's a pretty good photographer and has her composition down flat. Still I think she probably has an unwholesome crush on me. I've tried to tell her that I'm not just too old, but I'm repulsively skinny, speccy, and I probably smell like a crooked cop's ashtray, but I don't think she's getting it.

Let's see, what else. I ate a baloney sandwich for lunch (with mustard, white bread—oooh yeah). I went to Squirrell and picked up some mail and art board. When I came home Melissa had actually made something edible—veggie lasagna—but she wouldn't let me have any, begging the leftovers-for-her-and-Rob's-lunches clause. So I ate another sandwich and was sad until Laika came out of her room stoned and we went to the 7-11 for nachos and juice. Then we went home and I went to bed and masturbated and fell asleep.

Today I went to work (nothing from J.), then went to the other work (the studio that Lucas and I rent which is directly upstairs from the main Squirrell offices, which makes it feel just like going to work at an office. I can't ink comics at home, though; I get distracted too easily). Lucas was there too, even though he usually does his pencils at home. I inked one page, thumbnailed another page, and listened to Lucas talk about his beautiful, wonderful, gorgeous, smart, funky girlfriend. Shut up, Lucas.

I just got home a little while ago and Laika gave me a chocolate-chip brownie.

I think I might be high. President expresses shock. Film at eleven.

Good night. Time to jerk off.

13 August 11:02 a.m.

I'm at work—hiding the comp book under my tech support manual whenever anyone walks by. It's taken me ten minutes to write this sentence. Fuck this.

1:28 p.m.

Lunchtime. What a semi-civilized notion.

If I had a car or a scooter I'd go to Triste for lunch. I don't know why. Besides the crack. At lunchtime it's an even more bleak place than it is at night—the sunlight coming in through the windows gives off a milky grey luminescence that makes everyone look like they're recovering from viral pneumonia. Instead, I'm in the bar downstairs from Link-Up having an over priced and understuffed sandwich, watching *Cops* on the closed-circuit TV. This show makes me so paranoid.

So what am I thinking about today? Mainly Link-Up. Tech support. The Internet. The Industry. The other poor schmucks like me, whose only crime is that we weren't geeky enough, early enough, to become hardcore geeks—programmers, system administrators, software developers. I'm bitter, yeah. I was a nerd, but I spent all my high school pimple years in the art room, stuffing Rapidographs down my pants and penciling superhero physique. How was I to know?

I'm getting kind of tipsy. I had a pink lemonade and gin, perfect on a sticky-hot day like this, with my krab salad sammich. Getting tipsy brings out my sense of injustice.

2:15 p.m.

"What kind of person works at Link-Up?" Well, there's me, M. B. Squire, sarcastic, voluble, my cubicle decorated with pages from R. Crumb comics and every postcard I can find of Isabella Rosellini. (That makes five, mostly European, postmarked. I had a pen pal.)

To the immediate left of me is Randy. He's pale-blond and stocky and really into Windows 95—I mean, really into it. He's engaged to some chick and they show no signs of actually getting married; I think they just get off on the anticipation, the ego trip of dangling the *possibility* of marriage over the heads of their single friends. No decorations in his cubicle.

Around the corner from me is Moll Malone. I love to write or speak her name—so eighteenth century! She sounds like an adventurer. She's actually a normal suburban woman with a long history of customer service positions. She's got a great phone voice and excels at calming angry, agitated customers (not a skill that I myself share). Decorations are family and boyfriend Polaroids, employee of the month placard, cute puppy calendar.

Richard and Dave across the room. They spend a lot of time off the phone talking about upgrades, sweet new hardware, whatnot. True geeks. Dave is squat, beefy, vaguely slovenly; computer-generated pinup girls and the drawing of Tank Girl I did for him in his cube. Richard is tall and blunt, probably strong as hell (but from what . . .?). I've drawn him a couple of times as a typical thug in my comic. Cubicle decorations kind of like a mixture of Moll's and Dave's.

Beth and Thomas are okay. They're on the other side of the room. Good support folks. I've never noticed what they have up in their cubicles—maybe I should go look.

3:00 p.m.

Busted.

Trace came by when I was standing over there talking to Beth. He helpfully informed me that I hadn't picked up a support call in forty minutes. He just slipped it in, subtly reminding us that he's monitoring us, watching our phone stats like a nervous nurse checking in on the vital signs of an ER patient. He's not even our manager; doesn't he have big business deals to occupy him? Why can't he just get on with the owning and let us grunts do our grunting?

Now I'm all agitated. Maybe I'll take my cigarette break now.

"Squire."

Trace had followed me, whisking away my cigarette exhale with a wrinkled hand. His eyes were like two beads of jet floating in custard. "Taking a break already?"

"Actually," I replied, "this is the time when my breaks are regularly scheduled every day. It was your idea to institute timed and scheduled a.m. and p.m. breaks—and a fine idea it was too." I smiled, showing him all my teeth.

His answering smile, like a shark's, nauseated me. It did not mean good things. "Actually, Squire, I figure since you wasted at least a half hour off the phone, you've forfeited your break for the afternoon. And just to be fair, could you stay on the phone for an extra fifteen minutes late this evening?"

"Uh, actually, I can't do that today, Trace—I have to go to Squirrell today. I'm scheduled to be there at five-thirty. I can't make it there in time if—"

I'm sure he knew I was lying. "You're a creative guy, Squire. I'm sure you can think of something to tell them." His wrinkled mitt smacked me on the shoulder, and my knees threatened to buckle. "And move away from the front of the building when you're smoking—we've had complaints. It's a write-up next time, Mr. Squire."

When I got back to my desk, while on a call to a know-nothing in Astoria, I sketched Trace on a another Post-It—the shifty eyes, eight arachnid hands, the claws dripping with gore. And the Jaws 3D smile. He held the head of an unfortunate supportnik between double rows of teeth. The end result was so perfect that I had to put the Astoria call on hold and laugh.

Moll came around, wondering what had me in stitches. I showed her the Post-it. Her face reddened and swelled, just a hint of a smile warping her mouth into a curly bracket. "Oh my God," she whispered, "you are such an asshole."

I grinned, shrugged, and went back to the call with a light heart.

5:28 p.m.

On the bus. Listening to *Heaven Up Here*. It's very bleak; makes me feel more lighthearted in comparison.

Drew great caricature of Trace. Moll liked it. She's kind of pretty when she looks like she's going to explode.

Thought of a new rock opera about relativity—"Einstein on the Bus." Old Al finds out the hard way that, when you're on a bus at rush hour and you're late, time is objectively elongated and subjectively compressed.

I'm trying not to think about that whole Rob thing. I did pay the rent, right? Dammit, I can't remember. Laika's brownie bulldozed my brain, perhaps permanently. "That's why they call it dope."

Off to get cocked. My boss at Squirrell Press is actually named Rooster. His parents named him that. Nobody knows why. We call him Cock. Cock Kaplan. It doesn't help that, in the right light, he does kind of resemble a penis. A penis in a polo shirt.

I used to wear my Squirrell Press polo shirt at first. I was proud to be part of the collective. We were vanguards; very young, idealistic doesn't even begin to describe it, and thrilled to find that our little venture into comics seemed to be going somewhere. Ten years ago Cock Kaplan had got some money from an insurance settlement and started publishing indie comics of his friends that had gotten dropped from their regular houses, or who had never been "really published" before. Three years ago, before I'd even graduated from college, Cock took a shine to my sixteen-page mini-comics, designed, drawn, Xeroxed, and distributed by hand (well, Mom sold a couple at her store). He fixed me up with someone like-minded, i.e. Lucas, and gave us just enough money to feel legit, but not quite enough to live on. We didn't care; our childhood dreams had come true.

By summer of '97, though, Cock Kaplan reassigned me to inking, giving the penciling duties, the *real* drawing part, to Lucas. It hurts. It isn't as though I've run out of ideas. But the trust-fund-supported Lucas can do art full time, and I can't, and the issues have been taking longer and longer to produce. Lucas's drawing style isn't completely dissimilar to mine, and in fact he'd studied my pencils for a good long time while we were both young and dumb and new. Lucas told me that he loved my pencils, that he loved the way I drew faces, reactions, expressions. I am, however, not so good at drawing interiors—rooms, walls, drapery, what have you. Lucas has most of a degree in architecture, and he can draw an archway like you wouldn't believe. The more "sensitive work," the inking, was given to me. Lucas's pencils are tight as hell. To change anything of his would be to throw the entire panel, the entire page, out of composition. And I'm just not very fast. I just have to bite the bullet and ink precisely over what Lucas draws, fixing his mark in stone. He's just really good. It looks like my work, only better and tighter. Damn him.

Squirrell's not doing bad, twenty titles, five of them profitable (mine being one of these), two of them really profitable, a quarterly, a nice business in T-shirts, and a seemingly endless stream of beautiful seventeen-year-old front receptionists. If we're lucky, they know how to make coffee and copies; usually they spend a couple of days talking to their boyfriends on the phone and doing their nails and reading glossy magazines, and then there's a new one in her place, sometimes with a different shade of hair. I used to love this place. Practically idolize it. I loved everything about it and I was a total Squirrell fanboy.

I now use my Squirrell polo shirt to wipe my face after I shave—it's softer than any of my shitty thrift-store-acquired towels—and I just smile with gritted teeth when every other artist gets to do the cover of the quarterly except me. I painted the cover of #1 (beautiful exquisite eight-color pointillism, psychedelic as hell, practically an optical illusion) but I haven't been asked back, supposedly because the first issue of the quarterly didn't sell half its print run. Was that my fault? Were people scared away by the mad pure vision I'd had one rainy day? All right, so I'm too good for comics. A lot of comic artists are. I have a degree in illustration, not advertising.

Fuck this noise. I'm here. Time to take my caning like a good little schoolboy.

"You were supposed to be here twenty minutes ago." Cock was shooting hoops at his miniature basketball setup on the wall. "We do have deadlines, you know."

"Sorry. I had to work late at my other job."

"Your 'other job.'" Said with a sneer. "Squire, I really think you should consider getting serious about your comics career. A man cannot obey two masters—well, he can, but he produces shit if he does. The quality of your pages has gone way downhill lately."

"Look, man, I can't live on what I make here. It's not nothing, and thanks for the page rate, but I'd be living in a cardboard box. I have student loans—!"

"My name's not 'Man'." Cock's eyes were nail-blue steel, and it was only the coldness in them that kept me saying out loud, No, your name's Cock, dickhead. "The fact of the matter is, you're late. I'd like to think we sometimes pretend to be professionals. Remember, it's your dime paying the rent on that studio; if you're not going to use it, you're throwing money down the shitter. Go see if Lucas is done with his last panel."

Lucas Listener was at the light table, tallish, muscular, hair so boring I don't remember what it looked like, nose almost pressed against the glass. "Laika called," he told me emotionlessly, tracing the drapery of a medieval gown from a photocopy.

"Really? Why?"

"Something about Robert going through your room."

"What?!" I grabbed the phone, palms sticky already. Melissa answered. "Melissa, was Robert in my room?" I yelped, my voice shattering like an adenoidal fourteen-year-old's.

"I don't know, Squire. Why are you so paranoid?" She sounded, as usual, disgusted.

"Is he there?"

"Yep."

"Let me talk to him." I ground my teeth through the crackle of static, a low hum of interference.

"Yello?"

"Robert, Laika called here and said you were in my room . . . um . . . were you?"

"Yeah."

"What the hell were you doing?"

"Looking for cigarettes. I was out and you owe me a pack. Oh, and I looked at some of your comic books. You've got a lot of valuable looking stuff."

"Christ!"

"What are you getting so freaked over? I didn't do anything. Oh, and Melissa says to buy toilet paper on your way home." He hung up.

I hung up the phone and slumped onto a stool next to Lucas.

"Why so sad, Brad?" he said.

"My housemates are turning on me," I said.

"Maybe you shouldn't be so paranoid," said Lucas. "It's really annoying to live with someone who's paranoid."

11:30 p.m.

Wow, I've written a shitload today. This diary stuff is addictive. My brain's all over the place.

I made Lise come home with me. She chided me (is that the right word? It can't be "chode") for being too much of a weenie to go home alone and beat the living shit out of Rob, like I want to do. I actually kind of like it when Lise teases me. It reminds me of high school when my friends and I all pretended to hate each other. It was far more easy to deal with than possibly fake emotional closeness.

I'm not a weenie. I am realistic.

Asshole Rob completely ransacked my room—half of my comics are out of their bags, strewn around on the floor, my bed all fucked up like he wrestled an alligator in it. Roblissa weren't even home when we got here; neither was Laika, though she packed her bong and left it in my room with a note that said "Life sucks. Smoke a bowl." Lise and I smoked it and didn't clean my room; instead we listened to Prodigy and read some of the comics, which I haven't done in a long time. (I almost forgot I had the full run of *Wimmen's Comix*; thanks again, Mom.) Too soon, though, Lise gave me a hug and went home. Now I'm listening to the Bunnymen and trying to put the world back in order. And failing.

some pray for heaven while we live in hell.

my life's the disease.

Amen, bro.

I spent the next Saturday afternoon at Cafe Trieste, downing cup after cup of coffee with heaps of sugar, nibbling very slowly on an oatmeal cookie, and sketching. My hands ached like hell from the marathon inking job I'd done the other night, but I had to keep drawing or they'd lock up entirely. I had taken home a test printing of the next issue of my book coming out; every once in a while, I'd take it out of my bag and look at it. I'd done the cover—Cabby, our hero, sitting in a La-Z-Boy chair with his eyes strapped open, screaming at a TV screen displaying grey slashes of static (I'd really enjoyed painting that). The caption, lettered by Lucas, read "A Clockwork Duck A l'Orange." It was a terrible joke, but whatever; I needed a script out the door. The interiors, though, seemed to be all Lucas—his ovals as opposed to my compass-perfect circles, his Cabby a skinny, lanky, slouching figure instead of the disturbingly cute, knobby-kneed, blank-eyed cipher I knew he actually was. I knew his work was sharper, and more commercial, but all I saw was how much the title no longer belonged to me.

I wrote into my journal:

8/16/97 I am ever more a supporting player in my own fucking saga.

I felt a thick lump rising in my throat, and let my pencil rest in the crease of my sketchbook. I left the whole mess sitting there—coffee rings, mug, plate with crumbs—and went to the little phone booth at the back of the café, trembling, making a desperate call.

"Hello?"

"Lise, distract me. Get me out of this self-inflicted hell."

"Oh, Squire. You're not trying to pierce your own nose again, are you?"

I couldn't laugh. "Huh . . . no. I'm at Triste and I'm *hating* it. God, what am I doing here?" I moaned.

She moaned back in sympathy. "You're finishing up whatever you're drinking, and you're coming over here. I'll make you a mocha and some ramen and then we'll go see a show."

Everything brightened. "A show? Really? Who? Where? How much?"

"Shack-O-Love, at the Caravan, three dollars, you owe me five drinks. Actually, we can get in free; Jo's working the door tonight, and she'll let us in. You're heard Shack-O-Love, haven't you?"

"I don't remember what they sound like—I was really drunk when they opened for Old Gold."

"Well, so were they. They're good—kind of rockabilly punk with washboard and stuff. So hang up the phone, and get yer ass down here. I'm firing up the espresso machine as we speak." She gave a handy blast of steam on the phone to demonstrate.

"You are made out of gold-pressed awesome," I said.

"I know," she replied.

So I hung up, packed up my stuff, put on my sunglasses, and walked out into the hot, smothery sunshine. I didn't have any sunscreen and the sun carved into my neck where it was exposed between my hair and my T-shirt. My long fish-belly-pale hands looked like alien limbs. Tanned trucker types looked at me with revulsion and turned away. I checked my fly, checked my upper lip for a coffee mustache. Nothing was amiss—it was my very person that revolted those pillars of society, those salts of the earth. I was a grotesque worm, a mushroom in the sunlight.

A bus came, vomiting orange exhaust, and I got on it and went directly to the back. I pulled my knees up to my chest and gripped my portfolio bag tightly to my chest, staring over it at the front of the bus. Old ladies, mohawked teenagers, tough guys in warm-up suits—they were all looking back and giving me glances that mixed disgust and impatience. By the time I got to the stop outside of Lise's apartment building, I was shaking, breathing hard, my palms greasy and slick on the plastic, textured leather, and I jumped out the back door of the bus, almost stumbling on the high curb.

"My God, Squire, you look like you just got buttfucked by a Nazi," Lise remarked. I staggered into her apartment and shut the door behind me, then leaned against it, panting.

"I shoulda walked; I shoulda walked; I'm an idiot; I should have never listened to you. The bus is a torture chamber." I threw myself full length onto her queen-size futon. The flannel sheets were full of the comforting smell of Lise, and I was so grateful to feel safe and relaxed that I began cackling hysterically.

"Wow. Oscar-caliber performance. I almost felt sorry for you for a second. Mocha?" She was wearing a perky gingham apron, and she held out a soup-bowl-sized mug at me with her head to one side.

"Like I need any more coffee." I took the mug and swallowed about a third of it at once.

"God, you have a big mouth." She pointed this out to me every once in a while. It was the first thing she'd ever said to me, during lunch in the lunchroom at Teddy Roosevelt High School, watching me cramming half of a tuna salad sandwich into my mouth at once. "Chill out. I'm just watching TV." She sat beside me, put a cigarette in one corner of her mouth and a joint in the other, and lit them with a single sweep of her lighter.

Lise's studio apartment was tiny but it had high ceilings and hardwood floors that made everything echo like a cathedral. There was a kitchen behind a nice little half-partition that was also a glass-fronted shelf; all of it was painted the whitest white, and she'd thrown cheap rag rugs at random on the floors, where they kept company with cast-off jeans, coats, shoes, magazines. The portrait I'd painted of Lise's mother was on the wall next to the window—Mrs. Ballard stared out wide-eyed and accusatory, her mouth set in a hard thin line. It wasn't a very friendly picture, but Lise assured me that it was accurate.

I finished the other half of the joint and then smoked my own cigarette, staring uncomprehendingly at the television—she was watching a home-shopping channel while she rubbed lotion into her paper-ravaged hands. I turned away from the TV and stared instead at the painting, into Lise's mother's acrylic eyes, tracing the little flecks of gray I'd painstakingly dashed into her Van Dyke brown irises. Before I knew it, I fell asleep with my sunglasses still on.

I awoke to the strains of Gustav Mahler. Lise was changing into a very short little dress with a fluttery skirt, dotted here and there with cigarette burn holes. She didn't notice me being awake; she was across the room in the kitchen area, fiddling with her bra straps, her underwear, sniffing her armpits. It was a gorgeous sight, really, and I got a very swift and abrupt just-waking-up erection. I turned over onto my face and sighed. "You awake?" came Lise's voice.

"Yep," I said into the pillow.

"You really conked out there for a while." She laughed. "You ready to go soon?"

"Yeah, yeah, gimme a minute." I got up and brushed past her to the bathroom. I knew Lise better than to think that she'd flip out if she saw me with a stiffy—God knows she'd seen enough of them before—but all the same, I didn't want her to see one that was actually caused by her, whether she knew it or not. I washed my face in cold water, put in some eyedrops until my contacts slid around pleasantly, and composed myself enough to emerge from the bathroom. Lise was lacing up her big boots, one unshaven, athletic leg up on a kitchen chair. I stared out the window at the orange sun setting over the trees lining Belmont Street, and concentrated hard, hoping to spontaneously develop telepathy, and tell Lise to kiss me using only the powers of my mind, or at least turn toward me so I could see her panties.

We took the bus downtown to the Caravan. At the club, Lise got a pitcher of beer, and we sat at a table across from the bar. We were way too early. We got bored waiting for the bands to start, and ended up having another pitcher and some shots of whiskey, smoking dozens of cigarettes. Before we noticed much, the club was completely packed with sweaty rock people, all of them shouting at the tops of their lungs. I have no idea what the bands sounded like, but Lise danced and I made sure I didn't watch her. Randy and Dave from Link-Up showed up, Randy with fiancée in tow. They drank with us and we all shouted at each other. I said something that I thought was funny to Fiancée (I don't remember what) and she pushed me. Then Randy pushed me. Lise pushed Randy, someone's elbow flashed in the darkness, and the next thing I recall was Lise and I outside on the sidewalk, leaning against the building.

"Fuck you guys," Lise said peevishly.

"Walking blackout," I whispered. I walked behind the bus stop, stepping into the rock-gravel of the parking lot across from the club, and threw up. Nothing much came up at first, then it was almost entirely whiskey. "Oh, Christ," I said.

"C'mon, Squire, let's just go to the party. He said we could show up as late as we wanted."

"There's a party? You didn't mention a party," I said weakly.

"Maybe you were asleep. Hey, still, somewhere to go, huh?"

After staggering down the street for several blocks, I began to feel a little bit more sober. "God, I hate the Caravan," I burbled.

"What's your co-worker's name . . . Randy, right?"

"Yeah. And the tanning-bed beef jerky strip is his intended, Jolene."

"Damn, Squire, you must want your ass kicked—do you know what you said to her?"

"No," I said, laughing.

"Don't even try to remember. You don't want to know. Maybe you should have some water."

The party was about twenty blocks away in Northwest. By the time we got there, I had sobered up considerably, enough to feel the octopus limbs of hangover already starting to lock around my brain. We lurched up a set of porch steps just to meet a herd of besotted people going the other way. "Hey Jonny—Jonny!" Lise blurted, dashing into the house where I lost sight of her. I sat down on a saggy couch, picked up an abandoned glass with something in it that looked like margarita, drank it, and then felt the drunk-sickness coming over me again. My fingertips and lips were numb. I sank into the couch where I sat and closed my eyes.

Lise shook me at some point. "Squire, it's okay if we crash here," she said in a whisper. "I don't have enough money for cab fare and we missed the last bus."

"Okay," I responded dully.

"You can just stay where you are, I guess."

I probably said okay again.

"You know what you said to Randy's girlfriend?"

I couldn't remember.

"You said 'you remind me of my ex-girlfriend—can I come in your mouth? I miss her.'" She sighed. "Real gentlemanly. I'll see you in the morning." I felt her tuck a scratchy blanket around me. I slid over to one side and turned my head sideways, so I wouldn't choke on vomit in my sleep. I was pretty good at looking out for myself.

Daylight was cruel, stabbing and bright, even filtered through the madras cotton cloth over the front window. From the light, it was sometime around noon. Lise had already gone. "She didn't want to wake you up," said the friend, Jonathan, a diffident queer guy with big round glasses. He sat elegantly and distantly in the wreckage of his apartment, as if the party he'd hosted was part of some other long-gone life. "There's some coffee on the stove."

My contacts were killing me. They hadn't yet fused to my corneas, so I took them out and roughed it, pawing around in a vaguely nearsighted blur. I'd left my sunglasses at Lise's apartment, assuming we'd be back there at some point. I drank the coffee and dragged myself to a bus. My black X-Men T-shirt clung to my body with a layer of alcoholic sweat. I wanted more than anything to be back across the river, at home, in the bathroom with the door closed, throwing up.

The next bus wasn't due for an hour. Buses on Sundays were the product of the Devil's workshop. I walked until I found a gas station, went into the bathroom, squatted unsteadily on the slick floor (unwilling to let the knees of my black jeans touch the sickly, damp tiles), and shot the coffee backwards out of my gullet into the porcelain bowl. It didn't help. There was nothing much more in me. I rinsed my mouth, grateful that there was no mirror, and lurched back to the bus stop. I considered going somewhere and getting something to eat, but I just wanted to get home and get back to puking. I promised myself I'd finish someplace nice; I deserved that, at least.

It was broiling hot by the time I got home. There was nobody there, although the door was unlocked, and I breathed a sigh of relief that at least nobody would witness the pathetic wreck that I was. I went to the kitchen and got a pre-emptive glass of ice water, then headed for the bathroom to begin my residence.

Laika's door was open. The room was empty; stripped bare of everything, clean, even, the hairballs and dust and marijuana crumbs swept away. She was gone, as if some supernatural force had simply sucked her existence up. I stood there in her doorway, stunned, my throat choking back the impatient bile from my belly.

I spent several minutes on the cool tiles of the bathroom, resting my face against the rug-like toilet-seat cozy, tapping my empty glass against the side of the bowl, but I wasn't sick anymore. I just felt dead, the venom expelled from me. I toyed with the idea of calling my mother, but I knew she wouldn't be able to offer me anything of help. Instead, I got my journal from out of my room, sat on the floor of the living room, lit a cigarette, and uncapped my pen.

17 August

Laika's gone. What the fuck.

No answer was forthcoming. No one came home; no sound came to me in the dead, still living room except the sounds of cars swishing by on the street outside the house. Eventually I got up, took a cold shower, swallowed some aspirin, and went to bed for a while. Writhing on the twisted sheets, I slept and sweated the rest of the alcohol out of me, awakening with a start in the ultramarine cool of evening.

I put on clean clothes, put on my glasses, and came out into the living room, rubbing my eyes under the lenses. Melissa and Rob were sprawled on the couch, watching Laika's TV. They'd rented some dull Julia Roberts movie and were knocking back shots of Southern Comfort. They didn't greet me or look up. "Where's Laika's stuff?" I asked them.

"With Laika," replied Rob, grimacing his shot down and holding out his glass for another.

Melissa topped him up. "She moved out," she said succinctly.

"What are you doing with her TV?"

"She sold it to me," said Rob.

"Sssh," said Melissa.

"She sold it to you?" I was shouting. "She *transacted* with you?"

Melissa glared. "You guys, shut up! I'm trying to hear this!"

The back of my neck prickled like an angry cat's. "It's exactly like every other freakin' movie you watch! You could recite it in your sleep!"

Rob stood up and grabbed the collar of my T-shirt, dragging me through the swinging door into the kitchen. "You're a real little shit, aren't you?" he growled, tossing me back against the counters. "What the fuck is your problem?"

"I just—I just want to know why she's gone." I was shaking all over, sweating again, cold this time. I could envision Laika being driven away in an unmarked van, her freckled face pressed up against the glass. *Laika Come Home* with a sad flute on the soundtrack.

"Don't ask me. I don't even know her that well. If you care so much, she traded me the TV for helping her move in my truck."

I narrowed my eyes. If he was telling the truth, maybe he'd tell some more. I wanted to satisfy my curiosity. "Why do you sleepwalk?" I asked.

"I don't," he protested.

"You were sleepwalking the other night. You told me you were going to kill me in my sleep."

Rob laughed and spit into the sink. "That's pretty funny."

"No, it's not. It's not fucking funny."

"I think it is," said Rob. "Now why don't you just shut up and be quiet while Melissa's trying to watch her movie. She's too good to you—you're a gutless little turd. And I might as well kill you in your sleep—nobody would care, except maybe your dykey friend."

I just stared at him, unable to think of anything to say. For one thing, I wasn't sure which dykey friend he was referring to—softly butch but totally straight Lise, or the actually homosexual Laika. I watched him go back into the dark living room and say something to Melissa, and she laughed and answered him in the same tone of voice. They both looked over their shoulders at me and giggled to each other. I wanted to scream at Melissa, "Did you know your boyfriend is a misogynist homophobe?" But I knew it wouldn't do any good. They were dead to me.

When I went back into my room, I closed the door securely, propped my chair against the doorknob, and shoved a pair of tennis shoes under the door. I sat on the windowsill and wrote.

9:50 p.m.

Well, isn't this just typical. Puke my guts out, spend all day getting home on the stupid bus, and then find out the only housemate that I can trust has just "moved out." Took off. Sold Attila the Construction Worker the television set, depriving me of the life-giving rays of *Star Trek* reruns. It's almost enough to make me laugh, but my sense of humor isn't that fucked up yet.

I guess I got dressed because I want to go out again. I'm exhausted. Where can I go? It's Sunday night. I'm not going to a bar because I am never drinking again until tomorrow at the earliest. Triste is closed. And if I leave, I'd only have to come back. I feel like packing up my bandana on a stick and running away to join the circus. And I can't face going out through that living room again—I can't stand to wonder what the hell they're laughing at. What's so funny? Is it the general Camus-like pointlessness of my life? Or is that filthy scarecrow that They Might Be Giants warned me about, following me around, parodying my rants and frustration? I guess that would be pretty funny. If I wasn't living it.

I grabbed my shoulder bag, put my journal and sketchbook, all my Bunnymen tapes, my Walkman, and my copy of *Understanding Comics* into it. I twisted into the gray sneakers I'd recently stuffed under the door, and worked the screen off my window, climbing up and out. I dropped down into the coarse gravel below, a much further drop than I'd realized. It was too far for me to put the screen back on the window—

besides, it had to be done from inside—so I scrambled up and cranked the window as far closed as it would go before my arms gave out and I dropped back down on all fours in the gravel.

Then I just walked, just to get away from them, to be *not there*.

Eventually I found myself at the front steps of Lise's apartment building, eerily lit by the yellow light of the leather shop's sign across the street. The hangover had stripped the strength from my muscles and I couldn't go any further. I could have taken the bus to Link-Up and slept in the break lounge, but I didn't have the outer door keys, and I could barely hold my head upright.

I buzzed.

"Who the hell is it?" came Lise's voice, fuzzy and thick.

"It's me, Squire. I'm sorry I woke you up. I know you have to work tomorrow, but I do too and I can't stay at home—I'm gonna end up in jail or something."

"Aw, Christ." She buzzed me in.

I found her in the dim light coming from stove lamp, wearing a white Hanes tank top and faded satin pajama pants. The room smelled richly of incense, dope, and feminine sweat—not a bad smell, all told. She smirked at me. "What is it now, Squire," she said.

"Can I please crash here?" I asked sheepishly.

"Sure," she said. She tossed her blankets on the floor, then grabbed another sheet from a crate of folded linens and wrapped herself in it. "I'll wake you when I get up. G'night." She flopped into bed again and closed her eyes.

I turned off the light, kicked off my shoes and my jeans, and settled on the nest of blankets on the floor, the hardwood pleasantly chilly against my hipbones. Only after I'd relaxed and stopped rustling around did I notice that music was playing—almost silent, humming on the edge of audibility, as if the melody came from the wood and the white paint itself.

18 August 8:30 p.m.

Break between TV shows. Lise is in the kitchen making rice, singing along with the Cure. We're both a little goofy on beer.

This is pretty cool. I haven't mentioned going home yet and neither has she. I'm still sleeping on the floor, but there's a piece of egg-carton foam that I can curl up on tonight. Today at Link-Up I was so sore and stiff that I couldn't handle almost any calls. I spent the day answering e-mail, writing to Juba, reading alt.gothic, and doing the crossword puzzle online. Nobody seemed to catch on—at least, nobody gave me any shit.

Must call my mother. I guess she's getting online now, but she can't figure out how to find anything. This damned older generation—making everything harder than it really needs to be. They should stop looking for explanation or interconnections— just do as the little manual says. Don't try to psych it out. Just obey. There's plenty of time for questioning and going out on your own once you know what the hell you're doing, but first, please learn how to double-click.

THINGS TO DO TOMORROW:

-Go home. Change underwear.

-Buy Lise some replacement ramen.

-Tell Juba to resend the attachment. It came through as text, and I was really annoyed.

-Figure out where Laika went.

-Get to grips with the ups and downs, 'cos there's nothing in between.

19 August, 1:12 p.m.

Lunchtime. Chicken in a pita. Pint of muddy brown stout.

I suppose Laika's in Seattle. Damn her. How could she leave me here alone? Her stupid girlfriend. I don't know what I'll do if I ever see her again. These betrayals I've been experiencing lately just blow my mind. I mean, I trusted those girls. I really did. We were a team, goddamn it; practically a family. Then Melissa meets Rob and turns into a fucking white trash bitch supreme, and Laika softens me up with brownies and then just takes off in the middle of the night. I can't believe it.

I need to start looking at apartment listings or other houses that I can join. God, I hate that part. L and M and I have been together for almost two full years; we got couches together; we bought bad art; we made coffee for each other. It's enough to make you puke.

At least Lise is cool with all this. We had a blast last night. We drank a four-pack of Mickey's and listened to the Cure until the upstairs neighbors hammered on the ceiling. Then we lay in our respective bedding nests and talked in the dark until something like three in the morning—mostly about high school and all the creeps who made our lives hell. I even remember the names of all the kids who made fun of me when I was little. She was impressed with how much detail I remembered. "Maybe you should cut that stuff out of your memory," she said. "You gotta get over it someday. Bitterness is a fatal poison." But I explained that bitterness was my only salvation. She seemed to accept that.

I really ought to go home. I skipped the underpants today. It's actually not bad. I feel like Jim Morrison.

11:45 p.m.

Lise has fallen asleep in front of the TV. I'm sketching her weirdly bent arms. I didn't go home. I really miss my art supplies. I take a pencil and sketchbook and an Onyx Micro with me wherever I go, but spare underwear just never made it on the list.

20 August, 1:00 p.m.

Lunchtime. Pizza and root beer. Chocolate truffle bar in my pocket, to be enjoyed with my afternoon coffee. A Squirrell night—dinner at Cock's, supposedly. Mrs. Kaplan—we know her name is Cindy, but Cock wants us to call her Mrs. Kaplan—if he was a dog, he'd piss on her to show his ownership—will probably make another really hideous go at *haute cuisine*, namely, dry chicken breast halves, a French-cut green bean, and a sliver of pickled ginger. No wonder she's skinny as a model (except for those amazing tits) and he looks like a Green Beret (with a ponytail). I wonder if she's going to wear those amazing red clingy pants again. Certainly it'll be another clingy lacy top so sheer you can see her red satin bra. Red lips, long blonde curls. Probably gives great head. Like I'd know what great head feels like.

Crap.

I feel quite low today, the truffle bar notwithstanding. No underwear, again. I can feel the seams digging into Mr. Frisky. My jeans smell funny. All of me smells funny. I like the white musk, but it doesn't quite go with my natural odor, which is something . . . well, I don't know. I don't know what I smell like. I know I like it, certainly. I wonder if girls find my smell sexy, or if they'd find me sexier if I didn't wash. Maybe I should have gone gamy today for dinner with Mrs. Cindy K., Mrs. Cock. She loves comic books, apparently. She loves *my* comic book.

10:20 p.m.

Thank God they have an upstairs bathroom.

Yes, a yucky dinner, though Lucas and I smacked our lips and made much of it. Lucas kept on talking about his girlfriend, really obviously. Cindy K. kept on looking over at me, sadly, sympathetically, her lips slightly parted to show a slightly crooked front tooth. She had her hair in a ponytail with one tendril left loose and trailing across her table-tanned cheekbone. She kept licking her fork and "yumm"ing, then looking pointedly at me. So I went upstairs and jacked off. Who can blame me? I wish I hadn't let out that little "ugh!" when I came, though. I went back to the table hot from exertion and Cindy K. asked me with sex-kitten innocence, "Squire, you're all red, is everything okay? Are you having an allergic reaction? The sauce does have peanuts in it—are you allergic to peanuts?" etc. etc. I had to flee before she brought out "dessert," which was something like kiwi sorbet. Run in fear.

I hope Lise has pot. I really need it. I'm starving, for one thing, and I could really use a couple of tokes and then a big bowl of oriental flavoring. *Real* oriental flavoring. Like out of a foil packet.

I hate Cock more than ever now. Before I simply distrusted him. Now I know he does shit specifically to fuck with me. "Where's your girlfriend, Squire?" he asked me in the middle of dinner, when I was dripping peanut-laden sauce down my chin because I was gaping at Cindy K.'s bared honey-baked cleavage so hard. So I instinctively told the truth, I didn't have any girlfriend, and Cock said "Who's that blah blah blah," and I told him that was Laika, who he'd seen at some industry party—I'd brought her because I had to bring a guest, and Lise had been visiting her dad in Vancouver. "I was wondering; she seemed a little out of your league," he said. What a shitty thing to say. Laika is not out of my league. Laika is a lesbian. A taken lesbian, at that. She's not even that good-looking, for Chrissakes. She's just thin. Bastard. I fucking miss her and Lise isn't my girlfriend.

19 August 1:00 p.m.

Lunchtime. Turkey, pastrami, provolone, pickles, dark rye. Best lunch I've had all week. Not enough left over for a beverage. Sitting outside, looking across the street into the window of Pronto. Lise inside, working one of the big copy machines. She's got her head down, staring at the surface. Walkman on. She looks exceptionally pretty today, wearing a dress under her polo shirt.

She nicely smoked me out last night and we stayed up late talking again, eating an entire bag of rice crackers. What a wonderful friend. I also called Mom today and she was also wonderful. Mom told me about her latest pot- and wine-soaked exploits with the Poetry Coalition—apparently they went skinny dipping in a pond and somebody called the cops. Nobody got hauled in, but there was much 'splainin' to do. I laughed so much that I got in trouble, and Trace called me and told me to get back to work.

I really must go home tonight. I really must. I'm sick to death of these jeans and this T-shirt. And Dave actually called me on wearing the same clothes four days in a row, like he's the fashion plate of the world. He's gonna get his. Whatever. I must make my peace with the world. . . bitterness is a poison . . .

Yeah, right, dude. Good one!

How did Jim Morrison do it? . . .

I had another weird thought that I can't seem to shake, so I'll write it down.

My mom tells me that my dad could never fail to get her to come. They only had sex something like five times, but it was always fantastic. Or at least, that's what my mother says. Seems to me like she was so idolizingly in love with him that when he was even vaguely sexually interested in her, she felt like the luckiest girl in the world. It kind of reminds me of the Angela/David Bowie situation, and mom agrees except that "Your dad isn't an asshole. David never cared a damn for Angie; he just wanted a mommy.

Jeremy honestly cares about me—well, cared." My mom still, every once in a while, describes him as if he were still alive. Sometimes she seems to think he's still tripping around Nepal being bored and gorgeous, instead of dead, really dead, reduced to ashes in an urn on a mantel in Stepney, next to a framed picture of Charles and Di and a candy dish of Malteasers. And Gran couldn't figure out why I wouldn't eat the Malteasers and instead spent the afternoon outside burning ants with a magnifying glass.

I thought of something else. Too many thoughts today. They won't slow down.

My favorite childhood game was making tents out of two chairs and a sheet. As long as we weren't expecting company, Mom let me set it up in the living room and "sleep out" in the makeshift tent. It was like a treat. I felt safe in there, buffered against the TV when I wanted the TV on, but everything showing was terrible; buffered against the sight of our dreadful apartment, my mother's exhausted face, worn out from working two jobs, going to school, and raising me—alone. Kind of like a Lifetime Channel movie of the week, just with a lot of pot smoking. She'd be played by Lily Tomlin, or maybe Sally Field, and I'd be played by Toby Maguire. Dad, in flashbacks, would be played by Donovan Leitch. I wish I looked more like that guy and less like an albino frog in a Mary Tyler Moore wig.

And now I must go back to work because I'm twenty minutes late.

Friday Lise and I met for lunch at the pizza place across the street. "I can't take it anymore. I've got to get home and put some underpants on," I groused.

"Chafing?"

"To put it mildly. It would be fine if it was a little cooler outside—but I feel like my johnson's been acid-washed."

"Ouch."

"Besides, maybe they've forgotten all about how much they hate me by now. Maybe they'll think 'Who's this nice stranger? We like him!'"

"There is always that chance," Lise drawled, picking the encrusted cheese off my paper plate and eating it like a monkey pulling grubs from a log.

"And I'd hate to overstay my welcome."

"That's the funny thing." She smiled. "I haven't minded it at all, actually. I kind of like having you around. Maybe I've lived by myself for a little too long."

"Maybe we're just getting old and complacent."

"You, maybe. I'm still full of spit and vinegar."

"That's 'piss and vinegar'. Get it straight, wench."

I actually did a good afternoon's work, and went in to Squirrell in a great mood. All I had to do that day was the cleanup work on our piece, since Lucas had taken the weekend off to go visit his girlfriend in Vegas. Cock hovered over me as I bent over my table. "Squire, don't take this the wrong way, but you smell funny," he said.

"Funny?" My good mood went out the window.

"Flowery."

"I've been using Body Shop White Musk shampoo," I explained, bending over the work again. His proximity was giving me a headache.

"Why?"

I looked up at him. He was giving me a confused, dubious look. "I've been staying with a girl, if you must know," I said.

Cock Kaplan looked relieved. "Why don't you get your own shampoo? Something neutral smelling. Like Head and Shoulders. You smell like a fairy."

I sighed elaborately. "Mr. Kaplan, all respect due, but I can come in here drenched in White Shoulders if I want. What does my signature scent or my sexual orientation have to do with anything as far as you're concerned? I'm here, doing my cleanup work, so we can get the quarterly out in time. Now, if you'll excuse me."

There was a long moment of silence, stretched tight and thin like a decaying rubber band. I began to regret speaking so freely, but I kept my head down, willing him to walk away, to forget I said anything, to have a sudden sharp blow to the head which would cause permanent and total amnesia, anything. He just kept standing there, as if waiting for me to say something else. "I want those boards on my desk in perfect—and I do mean *perfect*—condition at seven o'clock or there will be serious consequences," he finally snapped, and then turned precisely and marched from the room.

I had my diary balanced and open on my knees, and I dipped a convenient pen into blue-black India ink and wrote:

Cock Kaplan sure has a military baton stuck up his ass for being an ex-hippie Hunter S. Thompson burnout freak.

Maybe he can't put it to his wife the way she likes it.

Damn it, I have a line from "Stars are Stars" stuck on my brain. Lise and I were listening to the Bunnymen last night while we did the dishes. It's not a very nice line, now that I think about it:

now we spit out the sky

because it's empty and hollow

all your dreams are hanging out to dry

It was the first thing on my mind when I woke up this morning. I know it's a sign from my subconscious, trying to tell me something. I carry this mental Ian McCulloch around with me night and day and I always listen to what he tells me. He's always right, no matter how painful the truth is. I realized this when I was finishing my thesis and I'd been up all night—when the mini-thins wore off, I dropped a half tab of acid to keep myself awake. I was listening to heaven up here and during the long freakout jam that bisects "Over the Wall" and there's the great line

I can't sleep at night

c'mon and hold me tight

to the logical limit

Mac practically howling. Pattinson giving heartbeat. De Freitas imbuing stuttery breath. Seargant just ripping the shit out of every string on that guitar. It's like having the marrow flayed from your bones. It was the most intense spiritual experience of my life. I really felt like Mac was my symbiote, that he needed me somehow, and I needed him. To survive. To exist. Without me, Ian McCulloch is just another package on the shelf, without identity or worth, and without Mac, I am just a blind and crawling fetus. Echo & the Bunnymen are my spiritual nourishment, my friend, lover, nag, even soothsayer—when I'm listening to the Buns, if I pause in whatever I'm doing or thinking or saying, whatever line happens next is completely appropriate to my emotion, or my situation. But who is the host and who is the parasite? Is it my marrow being sucked or his?

Christ, Cock again. What have I done to deserve terrorization by the human penis

[The "s" trails in a big messy torn scrawl off the edge of the page.]

8:35 p.m. (approx.)

I finished. I'm on the bus now, listening to "Seven Seas." Feeling cheerful. Maybe I should stop being such a turd and try to get my personality together. From now on I vow to stand up to bullies like Rob and Randy, force their stupid girlfriends to stand up for themselves. I'm going to try to be more patient with customers on the phone, and with Cock Kaplan, and with Lucas. They're just doing their thing. It's not their fault that they couldn't possibly understand me. Nobody could ever know what goes on inside my mind.

Especially not Melissa and Rob. When I think of the way we were before, not so long ago, it doesn't even seem like the same people. When did I get so small and peevish? When did Melissa get so . . . boring? So normal? Was it that one party when they met? How would any of us have known? It seemed so innocent ... mistletoe . . . mulled wine . . . Creedence Clearwater Revival . . . They were dancing and then they had just disappeared. She dragged herself home at noon the next day with stars in her eyes, just about bursting because she couldn't brag about what a giant cock Rob has. I've heard her go on about it on the phone to everyone, but I wouldn't care and Laika wouldn't care—she's never fucked a guy in her life and doesn't want to. Laika. I miss her. I miss her braying- donkey laugh and her insistence that every once in a while, we get stoned and play softball catch in the park. I used to really like that. Melissa would come, sometimes, before.

Okay. Everything's going to be all right.

I got off the bus in front of the house. There was a smallish rented Dumpster in the driveway. I imagined it full of leftover Melissa horror food. Stuffing the diary back into my shoulder bag, I walked into the house, whistling cheerfully, ready to give them the full blast of reasonable Squire charm. Nobody was in the living room, so I went to the bathroom and took a piss and fussed with my hair in the mirror for a bit. Then I opened the closed door of my bedroom.

There was basically nothing in it. The milk crates in which I stored almost everything I owned were empty, and half of them were missing. My futon and futon frame, my banker's lamp and cheap art table (and the art supplies therein), my bookshelves, my boxes of rare and valuable comic books—all gone. My closet was empty except for a pair of holey long johns on a wire hanger.

A single photograph lay face down on the bare floor. I bent at the knee and picked it up. It was the picture of my mother and father in Mexico, the color picture, my father staring straight into the camera, his pale eyes drilling accusingly into me. I straightened up and slipped the picture into the back pocket of my jeans.

I must have stood there for a long time, because when I turned around, Melissa was leaning in the doorway, a self-satisfied smile on her face. "Where's my stuff?" I asked, my voice strangely neutral.

"We sold it," she said matter-of-factly.

"You sold it."

"Well, the house got broken into. Some little asshole didn't put the screen back on his window right and some thug came in and thugged a bunch of our stuff. My stereo. Robert's CD player and Walkman and his CDs. The TV." She bobbed her head towards me for emphasis. "We didn't know where you were, or whether you were coming back. Besides, you didn't even pay rent this month—what the fuck were we supposed to think? We sold your shit so we could cover our losses. The rest of the crap, we gave to Goodwill or we tossed it. And we had to rent a Dumpster. So we had to pay for that too."

"My bike?" My voice, still dead. "My comic books."

Melissa shrugged. "Your bike got ten bucks. And we sold the comics to some dude who works at a comic book store. We got a thousand dollars for them. I can't imagine why anyone would want them."

"A—A thousand dollars? Do you have any idea what those comics were worth?" I felt energy shooting forth out of the top of my head, achieving a kind of kundalini of rage. "I was going to retire on those! All my Toth! And you sold them for a thousand fucking dollars! To cover three hundred dollars in rent! So where's the rest of the money?"

Rob loomed over Melissa's right shoulder, the two of them filling the doorway, cutting off my only escape. It startled me how huge he was—six feet and then some, all vein-popping muscle, aggressive pork-fed fat, thick Cro-Magnon eyebrow ridge. Goose pimples leapt out all over my suddenly icy skin, and I looked at the window for a possible out— unfortunately they'd put the screen back up and nailed it shut. "We spent the money, fuckface," Rob said. "You got a hearing problem?"

"I can't believe this . . ."

"Believe it," Melissa said lightly, turning and walking out. I heard a stereo start up, playing "Magnolia Rose" by the Dead. The sound quality was excellent.

I tried to pursue, but Rob stepped in front of me, folding his arms. "Where do you think you're going?" he said.

"I'm going to talk to my housemate, if you don't mind."

"I do mind," he said. "She doesn't want to talk to you anymore. Anything you need to tell her, you can tell me. She's sick of talking to you because you don't fuckin' listen."

"You don't even live here!" I shouted.

"Since when? Who paid rent this month and who didn't?"

"Fuck you," I said.

"Fuck *you*, you little faggot."

"Melissa!" I tried to yell over the Dead. The music got louder.

"See? Why don't you save us both a lot of trouble and—"

"Go fuck yourself!" I snapped, and ducked under his armpit. The stench of his androgens nearly choked me. I went to the doorway of Melissa's room, but she kicked the door closed.

I went instead into the kitchen and pocketed my Bettie Page fridge magnet. They couldn't have that. I took out my keys and struggled to get them off the ring.

"The rest of your shit's in the dumpster," said Rob, leaning against the doorway. "I recommend that you pick it out and get the fuck out of here, before we call the cops and get your ass trespassed."

"I'm not a faggot," I said quietly. I didn't look at him. He stood aside to let me leave.

I went outside. The full moon beautifully illuminated an Edward Hopper-esque tableau of utter failure: the rust-colored Dumpster, the yellow printing on its sides, the cracks in the pavement, the smudged toes of my tennis shoes. I climbed into the Dumpster and caught sight of my trashed and broken futon frame, broken window glass, more underwear with holes, the pictures from my walls, and my box of photographs, partially scattered out and dulled by dust. Clothes, shoes, music, and most art supplies were gone. I dug out what sketchbooks that hadn't been ruined by broken bottles of ink and shoved them into my messenger bag, and started on sorting the photos. I recovered the other photograph of my father, a picture of my mother alone, Polaroids of my American grandparents, pictures of me and Lise when we were high school, a live photo of the Bunnymen taken by another pen pal, and a picture I'd taken of Amanda, my girlfriend in high school. I put them all in my bag except the picture of Amanda, which I let twirl back down into the dry gutter. I'd let that be over.

I had a sudden all-consuming craving for a drink, a pang so strong that it gave me a stomach cramp. Lugging my overstuffed bag, I slouched into the Bob 'n' Barrell on 37th and Belmont—the bar that I usually walked past with a mock-shudder—and sat down at the bar. The place smelled like beer, CornNuts, and vomit (or maybe just vomit). The bartender, a wretched hag of ambiguous age, wearing a Blazers sweatshirt and a red bandana tied inexpertly around her head, silently eyed me with plain distaste. "Give me a shot of gin, straight," I said after a long pause.

"Can I see some ID?" Her voice was a ruin.

"I'm twenty-three," I groaned, my voice rising somewhat with impatience.

"Sure you are. You look like a twelve-year-old. ID or no drink."

I fumbled out my Washington driver's license. She looked me up and down, then looked carefully at my drivers' license, holding it up to the light, flicking the edges to see if they'd separate. "Michael Squire," she read. "Height, five feet five inches, weight, one-eleven. Ain't barely nothin' to ya, huh? Ooh! Organ donor."

I rolled my eyes and lit a cigarette, tapping my nails on the bar.

The hag humphed, satisfied, and squirted me a shot of plastic-bottle gin. "I still don't believe you," she said to me playfully.

"I don't believe you, either." I pulled my journal out of my bag and slapped it on the bar.

Most of what I wrote is incomprehensible. There are at least four full pages crammed full of an EKG-esque scrawl, and one page of scratching when the ink ran out of the page. The legible words aren't really much better—I was drunk almost immediately.

Fuck fuck fuck fuck fuck my precious first printing *Love and Rockets* #1 and my *X-Men* #162 and my oh my god what the hell why the fuck does shit like this always have to happen to me why the fuck can't somebody else take the blame once in a while why the fuck are all these people out to get me? What did I do to them to make them hate me so much? I'm sorry I was ever born if there was some way to get out of it I would I'd go back in time and tell mom to use a prophylactic

hate

hate

hate

everything that's ever existed especially this gin which sucks dingleberries off my ass—where's that old scruffy bitch I'll make her give me another one

That makes three

That makes four

That makes ~~six~~ five and I'm out of money so I have to stop fuck where do I sleep tonight—in the park maybe—but then I'll be killed and robbed and raped and they'll take away my pictures and my Rapidograph so I don't want to sleep in the park at least not Laurelhurst Park which is home to the real life actual crazies and not people like me who only toy with being insane so where do I ~~do~~ go? It's still early and I have a quarter and a dime left so lets see oh shit the old bitch is getting mad at me because I keep laughing and falling off the bar stool oh shit this is actually pretty cool, actually the best night of my life ...

bopsie waddy waddy shake your money

[etc.]

There's a dark smudge of dried blood on the page. First of many.

"Lise!"

"Squire, is that you? What the fuck's the matter with you, dude?"

"H-h-help me?"

"Help you?"

"I'm fucking drunk and I fell down and I . . . like . . . fuckin' skinned my knee and my hands and it like, hurts, can I come in and like, rinse the dirt off?" My whining was repulsively pathetic. "I got kicked out of the house."

Lise's groan buzzed through the speaker grille on the front gate. "I'll be right down."

She burst out the front door, wearing nothing but a T-shirt and panties, waving her hands agitatedly. "What's goin' on?" she asked, unlatching the front gate.

I slid in and sat heavily on the front steps. I slid my hand through my hair, and the raw skin snagged. "Ow!"

"You're all bloody. Jesus. Get inside."

She led me inside and stripped me of my T-shirt and jeans. She cleansed the scrapes on my knee and my hands with a very soft wet washcloth, gently digging gravel out of my palm, leaving beads of dark blood. I sobbed my tale of woe openly and drunkenly, complete with flowing tears. "And then the hag threw me into the street," I concluded, gulping back juniper-flavored mucus. "I almost got ran over by a fire truck."

She shushed me quietly and smoothed my hair and dabbed the salt from my face. When she was done wrapping all my hurt parts in gauze, she hugged me and tipped my chin upward so that I was looking at her. I had stopped crying and my eyes were sore and empty; I was full of an almost pleasant, weary apathy. It was over, and I was safe now. She smiled. "I guess you have to buy some new underwear tomorrow, huh?"

TWO: Squire Takes Love In Stride.

1 September, 7:30 p.m.

So it's the first of the month, and for the first time in ages I don't have to pay rent to Melissa—instead I just wrote Lise a check for $250. Fifty dollars savings on the room in the house (which wasn't all that goddamn nice anyway) and all the peace of mind money can't buy.

Lise is on the futon at my feet, stretched out on her stomach, watching *Jeopardy* and lighting a joint, wearing a huge Madness T-shirt and jean shorts. She is a longtime ska, dub, and rocksteady fan. One of the photos I saved is of her at a Specials show, shaven head, dog collar, puffy black down jacket, and plaid miniskirt. That was her in tenth grade, shortly after I first met her. I thought she was ugly and fascinating, being much more into that kind of tiny waifish dark-haired goth girls—in other words, female versions of myself.

Mom is way into the idea of us living together. Now she doesn't have to make two separate phone calls to talk to her kid and her best friend. How economical. Lise and my mother talk on the phone all the time. I try not to eavesdrop; it's not very rewarding when I do. Clothes, books, the foibles of men and of people at work. Normal conversation, easy to tune out.

I bought another roll of egg-carton-foam for the floor; right now it's so hot that the lack of blankets is a blessing. Thank God I had all my Bunnymen albums on me. I really miss my other tapes. I wonder what they did with my mix tapes—you can't sell those. Or can you? (They were really good.)

You know, I don't care. I'm so happy to be out of that place that I wouldn't go back to save my life.

This is good weed. I'm getting kind of sqiuddly. Maybe I want to draw now. I haven't started on the next script, either. I haven't been writing much of anything, actually. The diary's been neglected. I feel kind of like the anonymous author of *Go Ask Alice*: Honest, I've cleaned up, no more smack, I'm going to be a good kid and appreciate my family and keep a new diary. Of course then Alice turned up dead of an overdose. I love that book.

Oh sweet—*Ren and Stimpy*! Lise has *cable*. I forgot. This rocks so hard.

2 September, ten to midnight

I just got off the phone with my mother. In totally separate but cosmically entwined circumstances, we were both a little tipsy (well, in my case, more than a little) and a little stoned (in her case, more than a little). Her poetry group are a bunch of wild people— my mom runs with a bunch of bad kids, where did I go wrong?— and they spend at least as much time drunk, shooting pool, lying out in the woods zonked in mescaline, as they do reading Sylvia Plath and Gertrude Stein.

When I think of all the subversive habits I got from my mother, it blows my mind. She takes drugs, but often only to enjoy really mundane and boring tasks, like gardening, cleaning the house, etc. Many was the time when I'd come home from school with Lise to find Mom weeping with happiness as she cleaned out the refrigerator. "Can you believe it, Bronwynn? Can you believe this crazy circle of life and death?" she'd gasp, holding up a very nasty and half-liquidated leaf of forgotten spinach. At first Lise was freaked out and got kind of anxious whenever she came over to our house, but one afternoon Mom just lit up a joint at the kitchen table (on her lunch hour, no less) and got both me and Lise good and baked. Then after she'd left, we found the rice crispy treats she'd made as a "surprise." After that, Lise wanted to come over every day. It was excellent. After school sometimes meant watching afternoon cartoons and eating Crackerjacks, laughing our heads off with my mom on the couch, handing us the bong.

I'm sure people would be horrified if they knew the way I grew up. Damn it, my mother's a verse-crazed beatnik; she lived a great, grand, tragic romance and managed to get through it with some kind of dignity. She gave me drugs for the first time because she knew I was curious, and she wanted to make sure that *she* knew if the drugs were good or not. She was my official taster, which meant that if I wanted to do acid, I had to wait until she felt like tripping and she could take some and see what it was like. Well, she did that at first. By the time I went off to college, I was getting my own doses and taking them when *I* wanted to. What a pathetic rebellion. I had nothing of the kind. Not much to rebel against—except maybe the Beach Boys, who I've never been able to comprehend. Oh well.

"Squire."

"Excuse me, sir, hold on." I punched the hold button on my phone, slid my headset down around my neck, and looked up. Trace loomed over me with a clipboard, squinting at the drawings of him stuck to the sides of my computer monitor. I glanced at the gallery. There were seven or eight of them now, of various levels of detailing from simple Schultz doodles to intensely shaded, crosshatched, stippled portraits, but all of them were unflattering to the extreme. "What's up? I'm in the middle of a bitch of a Mac call," I added innocently.

"Oh, are you now. Sounds to me like you were talking about the best place to get cocktails."

I had been. The customer was a twenty-seven-year-old guy in Camas, thinking about moving to Portland, and really into Manhattans and martinis. I was letting him know that the Cazbar was great at martinis, but their Manhattans were like brake fluid. "It was just a way to get him relaxed, so . . . uh . . ." It was no good. Trace stared at me like I'd just eaten his baby.

"You seem to put a lot of work into these," he said, flicking one of the Post-Its.

"Um, yeah, I do them when I'm on the phone. It's just practice. I can't really help it."

"I just came to tell you that you have your annual employee review on the twentieth. It might really help if you'd put some extra effort into your appearance, just for that one day, just to show me that you can, if you wanted to."

I was wearing what I always wore, that is, a faded black T-shirt (printed with *Primus—Suck on This*, bought for eighty-nine cents at the Goodwill the day after I moved in with Lise), rather faded black jeans (five bucks, same Goodwill), and gray canvas fake Chucks. I hadn't gotten around to buying many more clothes, since it was hot and the last thing on my mind was buying sweaters and nice wool slacks and Oxford shirts. "Um, okay," was my response. "Thanks for the reminder. I've got this guy on hold, so . . ."

"So get back to what you're getting paid for," Trace snapped, giving the Post-Its one last sneer and turning to his next victim, Moll, who visibly paled when he walked up and tapped her on the shoulder.

After work, I went to the Salvation Army to look for nice clothes, but everything I liked was too big for me—the perennial problem in my life. I didn't want to spend forever shopping out of the boys' section—I mean, at least when I was wearing all black, I looked something like an adult, or at least a college kid. I stood in front of one of the mirrors holding up blazers against myself, not really seeing anything except the chapped lips, glasses, and the raspberry-red roseacea stains on my cheeks that my mother called "my natural blusher." Several days' growth of hair stained my upper lip and chin, but it mostly just looked dirty. I looked like a boy playing Dress Up In Daddy's Clothes.

Before I knew it, the store was closing and they kicked me out. I wandered around Grand Street for a while in the hot, murky dark, looking for stars in the sullen sky, sucking down air pollution, smoking and humming songs. A homeless guy asked me for a cigarette; I was running low, so I said no. Almost without pausing, he called me a "fuckin' asshole" and kept walking.

I walked the rest of the way home, enjoying the cooler air of evening, to find Lise and her friend Elizabeth on the futon together, drinking bottles of beer and watching a movie. "Hey, Squire," Lise said. Elizabeth burst out laughing.

"Hi," I said, going to the fridge and taking out the cold-water pitcher. "What's so funny?"

"Nothing," said Elizabeth. "I should get going, Lise."

"Yeah—okay—let me know about shopping tomorrow."

"Do you want to come to the show?"

"No, I have plans. Remember?"

"Oh, yeah. Totally. Well, bye—see ya, Squire." Elizabeth's voice became a drawl that was supposed to be suggestive, but mostly just made her sound like a drag queen.

"Bye," I said, not looking up until I heard the door close. "So, not to be paranoid, but what were you laughing about?"

"That's paranoid, Squire," Lise said, frowning, then smiling and sticking out her tongue. "Now, grab a beer and some dinner. They're showing the first three Star Trek movies, and we're only half-way through *Wrath of Khan*. And Liz brought over some killer bud. Ah, there's that smile."

4th September, 1:13 p.m.

Juba has me tripping. I had to print this out:

[this, printed out, glued into the composition book]

My most beloved Squire,

Summer is hell. SO BORED. There's got to be some way I can get addicted to crack or something. There's no crack in San Sabas as far as I can tell, just a lot of idiots who think that being a debutante is actually a really good thing. What kind of brainwashing did they have? Anyway, enough of that. Arachne and I waxed our legs—what a rush! Worth it, too. You should try it sometime. Arachne's boyfriend is coming back from Chicago day after tomorrow and apparently they are going to have sex for the very first time. She's already rehearsed what she's going to do and say—she's definitely going to give him a bj. She was kind of iffy on it, but I told her she has to do it for Science to see if it's really gross or what. If she doesn't like it, I have to buy her lunch for the first month of school.

Now if I can get my parents off my back about this debutante thing, I'll consider myself to be doing something right. They obviously don't know me at all if they think I'd be into something that stupid—I mean, all that money that I'd really rather spend coming to visit you and show you the tattoo that Arachne gave me. I would take a picture of it, but it's in such a weird place and I don't think the camera would reach.

So when are you coming to see me? You do like me, don't you? You should come for my birthday—sweet sixteen. I think my mom is making a cake with swoops of pink frosting and silver decorettes. Dear Gaia. Arachne and I intend to play along until midnight or so, then we're going downtown to drink Jäger and try to stir up some trouble. She just got the freshest pair of leopard-skin thigh boots out of this catalogue and she looks really hot in 'em. I will take a picture and send it to you.

This picture was something we did last night. It really looks like it hurts, but it's actually pretty comfortable—she stuck a pillow under my neck so I could relax. Don't you think she should become a photographer?

...Juba...

"I am human and I need to be loved just like everybody else does"

The accompanying picture is just way too intense. I waited until everybody else had gone home before I even looked at it, and I'm glad I did. She's right, it really does look like it hurts, and yes, Arachne has a long future ahead of herself as a photographer for *Hustler*. She's not as good as Juba, but she could probably get work.

I e-mailed her back and told her that yes, I did like her, but that I didn't think I could make it out for her birthday. Am I leading her on? Man, it's kind of exciting—I mean, she's seen pictures of me; what does she think she's doing? Why would anybody develop an unreasonable attachment to a broke guy who looks like a cross between a sparrow and a frog? But whatever. It's good for my ego. I just wish that real girls would actually take an interest every once in a while. Since Amanda, I think I've been on like three dates, all either boring or disastrous (remember Julia? And the shellfish? Yeah). Amanda really fucked me up in a lot of ways. I just don't even know if I can actually have sex anymore. What was it like? I just remember it being really, really nice, if a little terrifying. It's a big trust issue thing, putting a part of yourself into another person. Like, *inside.* But I really enjoy the kissing and snuggling part, and the soft sleepy feeling that comes after you've come, which I actually do get to feel on a regular basis. Or did. I can't really jack off with Lise in the apartment, which is kind of a drag, so I've changed my schedule to daytimes. I usually get my rocks off right at the end of my lunch break, which makes going back to work really difficult. It's also hard to visualize a horny goddess fingering her slick open pussy while you're standing in an echoing, cold metal stall. Oh well. Maybe I should just ask Lise if there's a good time when I could get off when she's not around. Would she mind? Maybe a note?

I returned from lunch, still licking the pizza from my chops and hoping to take a few minutes for my daily constitutional, but Beth grabbed me in the hall and dragged me towards the support office. "Meeting, Squire, meeting; did you forget? Trace is going to ream your ass for this," she muttered under her breath.

The support technicians looked up as one as I came in. Gently I eased myself down onto the carpet, at Moll's feet—the safest place from a psychic standpoint. We always sat together at meetings, so we could trade knowing looks.

This staff meeting was almost exactly like every other. Words careened around the room—words that meant nothing to me, like "proactive," "morale," "retirement benefits," and "Solaris." Grievances were aired. Beth actually raised her voice. All through it, Trace just sat there and watched all of us, warily, as if expecting a gun to be produced at any moment.

"Certain members of the support team haven't exactly been pulling their weight," said Trace when he finally spoke, stretching like an anaconda contemplating lunging for a suckling pig. "Of course, Moll has baby Kellie, and Thomas has his back injury, and Squire..." He glanced over at me and bared all his teeth, even the molars. "Of course, Squire has his *other* career which obviously means more to him than Link-Up does."

There were soft sniggers of laughter. I took a deep breath and looked past Trace's left ear to the wall.

"What I have to say doesn't come easily. I'd love it if we could have a free-wheelin', nice and easy approach to technical support. But we can't. Our competition is very professional. They don't have the sheer technical skill that we have, of course, but they treat each customer as a priority individual. None of this 'Sorry, I don't have an answer for that, and I'm not crazy about your tone of voice, ma'am' stuff. Squire."

"There was nothing else I could do," I blurted. "She was insulting me. She was getting personal. I told her there was nothing I could do about the stupid T1—if I could have crawled down there and spun fiber-optics out of my ass, I would have."

More sniggers. Moll poked me with her toe.

"That's all right, Squire. But at the same time, how would you feel if you were that person?"

Of course the obvious answer was "I wouldn't give a shit," but I had the feeling that wouldn't fly. I shook my head and looked at the carpet.

"Exactly. We have to be professional. We have to take Link-Up seriously. We're on top, but we won't stay there without your help . . ."

After the meeting broke up, we all slumped back into our ergonomic chairs and reapplied headsets to our skulls. I didn't immediately put myself back on the phone, though. I let my hand hang over the button for a full ten minutes before I pressed it and let the meaningless words spill from my mouth—"Link-Up Tech Support, my name is Squire, how can I help you today?

5 September, 11:22 p.m.

I'm getting stoned and I'd rather be drinking. No booze in the house. Lise traded one of her co-workers, a seventeen-year-old high school dropout, all of our vodka and our whiskey and all our gin for this huge bag of Oregon buds. I see the wisdom of Lise's decision now, but all the same, I need to get fucked up and I'd rather be drinking my way there.

I'm getting stoned and I'd rather be drawing. I got a new pen today and I want to see what it looks like on my troublesome recycled paper.

I'm getting stoned and I'd rather be . . . making daiquiris. Banana and melon daiquiris. The get-chicks-into-bed strength daiquiris. The kind of daiquiris that will make Lise shed her tough-gal exterior, rip off her black lace tank top, and devour me. Yeah. I want daiquiris.

I'm getting stoned and I'd rather be reacting to people emotionally—the kind of emotionalism released by alcohol. Pot doesn't have any emotionalism. It brings either clarity or a cloud. Nothing in between. At the moment I'm realizing clarity. My repressed desire for Lise is making its way to the surface again. What the truth is, Squire, is that you're starting to dig her again, the way you swore you wouldn't. Remember the time you couldn't even look her in the eye for a week after you called to ask her on a "date," and you chickened out and hung up on her? Remember how you listened to her conversations with your mother through the walls, just so that you could hear her voice when you jacked off? You thought you buried all that. You didn't. Quit kidding yourself, baby.

I'm getting stoned and I'd rather be getting laid.

I'm getting really stoned and repetitive. Just a little bit. I really wish I'd gotten drunk instead. I have enough stress in my life already without looking at Lise's feet every night, wondering what they taste like.

Lise home. She got more liquor, oh, bless her. She's pouring a really stiff shot of gin in a tall glass, dropping in ice, and shoving an olive on top. "It's a fucking martini, Einstein, a fucking dry martini," she says. "You're welcome."

Shortly after, there came that Sunday afternoon. I never did forget that, and I doubt I ever will.

The blistering heat of the last week had mellowed to a nearly pleasant Crock-Pot intensity, and there was nothing on cable more fascinating than the Weather Channel. I had worn one of Lise's tank tops on Friday (a winsome number, pale green with a Bee Gees sparkly iron-on) and had gotten a really bad sunburn. Friday night and Saturday had seen me lying face down on the futon, wearing only boxers, reading graphic novels while occasionally slathering my neck, shoulders, and arms with aloe vera. Lise had to cover some shifts at Pronto, without protest, grateful for their air conditioning. Sunday, though, we'd spent the day drinking beer, eating popsicles, smoking some of the new weed, and watching a tape of Voltron episodes she had gotten at a yard sale.

The tape ended. I assumed my former face-down position on the futon, head dangling somewhat over the side, and Lise put on some music. She opened another beer. "Want another popsicle?" she asked.

"No, I'll hurl."

"Hmmmm . . . can I put some more aloe on your back? You're looking kind of peely-snaky back there."

I looked at her ankles and feet, crossed casually, bare, one big toenail gently scratching a mosquito bite on the opposite metatarsal arch. I bit my lip and said casually, "Uh, yeah, sure; it's in the fridge."

I stripped off my shirt, closed my eyes and lay as still as I could, trying to control my breathing, trying to make my heart stop beating so quickly. My fingers were sticky with popsicle leavings, but I left them dangling on the ends of my pink peeling arms. When a stimulus came it was shocking—Lise's hands, cold with aloe, moving with excruciating slowness on my sensitive back. I gasped a bit. "Sorry," Lise mumbled.

"No, it's just cold. Feels pretty nice, actually."

"Well, good." Her hands became more brisk, slathering me heavily with the slick aloe, then began to work in earnest, rubbing it into my skin. "You're so skinny, child," she declared, flicking her fingernail against my shoulder blade.

"I try to be fat," I protested, and we both laughed.

"You eat enough junk food. I've seen you."

"It's my nervous energy," I said.

"That much is obvious. You have enough neurotic energy to fuel the southeast grid. And maybe then some."

"Am I neurotic?" I asked pleasantly.

"Are you neurotic. Are there hicks at a bait store? You set new records of neurosis, pal. Whole new schools could be set up just to study how loopy you are."

"And why do you put up with it?"

"I don't know," she said. "I guess I kinda like you."

We both stopped breathing for a second.

I turned over and looked up at her, and she bent over and kissed me on the mouth, her lips sweet with lager and sugar. Her breasts brushed my collarbones, then she was pressed up against me, all the delicious weight and smell and skin of her, sweaty and smooth, and her heart beating quickly against mine.

62

September 6th, 1:04 a.m.

So there is love. There exists love. I assumed, having given and received Valentines before (admittedly, receiving far fewer than I gave), that I understood love, that I had been "in love." Nothing of the kind. Love is not a state that I myself create or destroy—it's a continuum, a medium, a sea into and out of which we pass. I have been dipped into this sea like Achilles into the Styx, and all of me but the tendon is made invincible by love.

I breathe in love—I exhale love. I feel like a mutant gene has been awakened inside me, like an X-ray shatters the helix and breeds a monster—the mutant gene that makes me run across the street for olives and malt liquor at odd hours of the night. Some would be shocked by the impersonal nature of love, but it's both universal and terribly individual, as every atom has its place, its significance, in a vast and uncaring cosmos.

Isn't it amazing how a kiss can just go on and on for what seems like ever? How your whole body is giving you demanding signals every few seconds—hurry up, I want to fuck, I want to fuck—but your mind and your heart draw it on for longer, enjoying the tension, the astonishment. Surely that happens only the first time you kiss someone—with Amanda I thought I'd explode with excitement after kissing her for five seconds, and we'd usually end up panting and covered with jizz fifty-five seconds later. This afternoon it was a long time of kissing, and then a long time of taking off each other's clothes (she had it easy, just some shorts and some jockeys, and all I had to deal with was a light dress and some knickers and that bitch of a bra with the closure on the front, which caused me no end of grief and my lady fair no end of amusement. (Vexation, I should say. Not grief. I was caused some vexation.) But once that was done with . . . Oh, man. I've forgotten what nipples are like. I mean, there's my nipples, which are small and pink and almost always hard, but they're not girl nipples, which startle me with their size, their springy firmness, their responsiveness. I thought my nipples were pretty sensitive—she pinched the hell out of them in fact—but if you so much as brush hers with your fingertip, she's humping your leg. That was great. I never had anything but a basset hound hump my leg before. It was much more exciting this time.

And she came. And she was sopping wet and horny afterward. And we fucked three times tonight already and I'm looking at her now, asleep on her side next to me, and I want to have her again.

She is so beautiful. Next to her I'm a peeling red monstrosity. She took great pleasure in ripping big peeling chunks of skin off my back—it both hurt like hell and turned me on. She is as icky as me. The floor is littered with bits of shed skin and the shed skins of condoms, glistening in the light from a candle. This is really bad for my eyes. I should put it down and go to sleep. But I have to get some of this love out of my system or I'm going to burst.

5:35 a.m.

Lise by dawn. Lovely, stinking of sex, smiling in her sleep. Mom is going to lose it.

". . . Put your arms around me . . ." I breathed softly down her neck, and she rolled over and obeyed me, eyes still closed, lips pursed as if she were trying to concentrate. I kissed her face and chest and wrapped my legs around hers under the flannel sheet. "Wake up; let's make out," I whispered. I was on fire with the desire to bring her to orgasm again. The sense of power it gave me was incredible.

"Okay," she replied, completely awake. Her dark sleepy eyes opened and focused on me, and she smiled as she reached down and grabbed my penis.

We had a long, slow, intense fuck with hair-pulling and screaming, me trying to pierce all the way through her and she seeming to want that as well. I felt half dead but exalted, having had no sleep at all, and something like twelve hours of semi-continuous screwing. Finally, I lay unmoving on top of her, still inside her, and she toyed with my hair and with a loose flap of skin on my shoulder, kissing me and sucking on my lower lip.

Abruptly, she shook me off. "Shit! You're going to be late. You've already missed your bus." She sat up in bed and agitatedly smoothed her hair down.

I sighed and looked at the clock. I heard, below on the street, the bus that I took to work rumbling by, and a second later I smelled its exhaust. "Fuck work," I said, turning over and burying my face in the pillow.

"What do you mean, fuck work?"

"I mean, *you* don't have to work today. I don't want to go to work. I want to stay home with you. I have sick days." I rolled over and grabbed the telephone receiver and winked at her.

"Link-Up; this is Trace."

"Trace, it's Squire. I'm not going to be able to come to work today."

"Oh, really?"

"No, I'm sick. I picked something up this weekend."

"What, the clap? Or the convenient 24-hour stomach flu."

"I don't know what it is. Maybe it's heatstroke. My head's killing me. I can bring you a note from my doctor, if you need some kind of proof—or maybe I should just in and puke all over my phone."

"There's no need to get smart with me, Mr. Squire. You've got sick days coming to you. All I have to say is that when they run out, you're gonna wish you still had them. For when you're really sick." He hung up.

I hung up. "Asshole . . ."

"What's the matter?" Lise asked, lighting a cigarette. She looked gorgeous and perfect, and not just because she was topless and in bed with me.

"Nothing. The deed is done; I'm off. You wanna go back to sleep?"

"Yeah . . . I wasn't ready to get up in the first place, but then, you and your lunging advances . . ." She laughed and snuggled down closer to me.

I took the cigarette from her, had a drag from it, and dropped the butt into one of the empty beer bottles on the floor. "It's not safe to smoke in bed," I said.

Lise smiled. "Okay, Woodsy Squire. Only you can prevent forest fires."

"I'm trying to save your life. I don't want to live without you."

It was the corniest thing I had ever said, but it was both true and utterly spontaneous. And she didn't mock me for it, either. Instead, she kissed me. We put our arms around each other and lay quiet, listening to the traffic outside. "I know you won't believe me, but you're a really great fuck," Lise said.

"You're right; I don't believe you."

"I always had a feeling you would be, as long as you gave a damn."

I squeezed her hand. "Thanks. I've done my homework."

"You wanna know when I fell in love with you?" she asked.

"When?" I responded. For some reason, though she'd used the illegal four-letter word, it seemed totally natural, as natural as it had been for me to write it in my journal. Of course she loved me. I loved her.

"When you brought the first issue of your comic in to be photocopied. You were so happy. And beautiful. I couldn't believe I'd never really noticed that before. And it was such a good comic. That story about the little doggy who's trying to quit smack, and his girlfriend leaves him? I swear to God, that broke my heart."

That was years ago. Absurd. As absurd as being called beautiful; hideous me. But I accepted it; in that moment, everything was possible. I smiled and rested my forehead against hers. I rubbed my thumb across her nipple, just to feel her shudder lightly against me. "You know when I fell in love with you, Lise?" I said.

"No; when?"

"This last Fourth of July—when we were watching fireworks."

She laughed. "Oh, man, I was tripping balls."

"We all were. But you just got this look of utter joy on your face—like you were on the side of everything that's good, and against everything that's bad. I watched the fireworks reflected in your eyes."

"Oh, Squire, that's lovely."

"It's true," I mumbled, embarrassed all over again. "I mean, I loved you before—I've loved you since pretty much the day I met you—but that's when I really fell in love."

"If we've been in love with each other so long," she sighed, "what took us so long?"

"Well, you were going out with other guys, and then I was seeing Amanda, and then . . ." I shrugged. "I don't know. We're idiots."

She hugged me against the softness of her breasts. "Yep," she sighed. "We're idiots. I'm glad you're here now, though. I guess everything happens for a reason."

6 September, late

Lemme get lyrical here for a second. I pity the rest of the world for not being able to have this right now—a backlog of pleasant remembrances of the way it was before, those royal long afternoons smoking pot and cigarettes, deeply ensconced in the vulva of the futon couch in Lise's living room, simply happy to be sitting with my best friend watching *Mars Needs Women* over and over again. And now, to be here, on that self-same futon only folded out into a bed, with this glorious person, marvelous Lise, my best friend and my lover. The rest of the world. They don't know.

Later . . .

What a grand day.

I mean really, does it actually get better than this? I sketched, napped, smoked, ate crab cakes, cucumbers with sour cream, and watermelon; I went for a walk around the block while it was still cool outside; I spent the hot part of the day asleep, waking up only long enough to take a sip of ice water and kiss Lise, lying half-conscious next to me. Spent the evening in a cool bath together, eating more watermelon and taking shots of vodka.

Lise looked at me all day with adoring eyes. I've seen her look at other things like this —mainly kittens. Her eyes are very large and very dark. Her mother was Greek and you can really tell sometimes—her mother is Greek, I should say. She still is. I always think of Lise's mother as being dead, but she's far from it—she just might as well be dead, she's so far away and has been for the entire time I've known Lise. Lise's dad is far away too. She never hears from her mother, and her father only communicates every once in a while. No wonder she latched onto my mother. My mother's enough Mom for two whole kids.

Lise is actually on the phone with Mom right now, telling her all about it. It makes me feel kind of squirmy—Lise isn't going into gory detail, but it's creepy for me to know that my mother even knows I've had sex even once. Lise is grinning at me, naked except for a chain around her neck with an eye of Horus pendant dangling right between her breasts. A thin, artistic line of dark hair runs from her navel over her rounded belly into the dark and curly crevasse of her pubes. It's like something out of Degas. I will never sleep with a blonde woman ever again. No, it's Van Gogh

I'm thinking of. The sketches of whores. Toulouse-Lautrec. Gaugin?

. . .

I just got off the phone. Mom wanted to talk to me. She told me that she's very happy for us, and that I have to remember to be responsible and generous. "Those are the important points of lovemaking," she went on, like she wrote the book. "Be responsible, be generous, and relax. Above all relax." Maybe she didn't know that I'd ever had sex before. I mean, how could you have not known about Amanda and me? I thought it was incredibly obvious—I had a perpetual erection around her for one thing, I only went to class when she blew me off, etc. She really did let me come in her mouth once. I couldn't believe her. I guess it was kind of erotic, but mostly it was just shocking—like watching someone drink blood. I think I only had actual fuck sex with Amanda three times—I came too soon about five times and eventually she got sick of it and gave me a very nasty, very public chewing-out about what a loser I was. I don't know, maybe ten people heard it, but in a relatively short time everyone in Bellingham knew that I was a premature ejaculator—everyone, apparently, except my mother.

Fortunately I am no longer a premature ejaculator thanks to constant and grueling work controlling my tantric urges. I simply redirect the energy through my cranium and it very nicely finds its way back to where it's supposed to be by the time it's due there. Like the lady says, everything happens for a reason.

After Lise and I got together, it became hard as hell to concentrate on anything else. I showed up at work hung over, still stoned from the night before, my dick sore from being prodded, yanked, and sucked all night, my hands cramped from grabbing and caressing every part of her I could reach. It physically hurt to sit in my ergonomically incorrect chair, eyes closed against the bluish glare of the huge monitor screen. I spent support calls in a half-reclining position, hand up my shirt, gently rubbing my nipples, directing customer after hapless customer through Winsock conflicts, bad system folders, web browser installations, and power-cycling printers. Once I came to at the end of a call to find Randy, Dave, and Beth staring at me like they were at a peep show.

My monitor was dripping with caricatures of Trace now; fifteen of them, lined up and arranged, meticulous, shading from the crude to the exquisite as you went from left to right, counterclockwise. I tucked some of the best of them into the diary; they genuinely are pretty good. I didn't want the sketches to be stolen when I wasn't there, which happened to the Dracula sketch; taken by whom, I never knew. Yet I didn't take them down. They were some of the finest artwork I'd done since I got out of school.

Each of my cigarette breaks tended to last for a half hour. I just didn't care anymore.

Moll. "Why are you acting like this, Squire? I mean, do you want the unemployment that bad? Not that you could get unemployment; you've got another job already."

Thomas. "Dude, this is amazing. But . . . Trace is gonna get you. I mean, this is libel, or treason, or something like that."

Dave. "Can you make me another drawing of Tank Girl?"

Beth. "Squire, please get back to work."

Juba: *It's too hot to wear clothes. Arachne and I drink lemonade all day long and yesterday we went to the water slides and some boy tore my bottoms off. I mean jesus christ he could have asked. Arachne's boyfriend wants to see our pictures, even though we told him that we only do it for you and no-one else. We trust you. We've read your comics. We know what kind of person you are.*

I actually got laid too—nothing so nice as what you've had. Lise sounds so wonderful. And I'm glad she doesn't shave; I admire that, and it's rad that you think it's sexy. I went to a party thrown by the rival high school, whose summer school baseball team just beat ours—like wow—and I got pretty drunk and fucked the valedictorian of the senior class. His name is Rick. His wanger is really small and he chewed on my lips until I felt like puking. We used protection, of course (just to reassure you! That seems to be all people care about nowadays—no "Did you enjoy yourself? Do you feel any different?" No it's "Are you going to die now?" whatever) but I didn't get wet until he was already done. He wanted to see me again but I told him no. I can't imagine going out for frozen yogurt with this guy when all I can think of is the way his butt smelled. You'd think—the guy has a 4.0 GPA—he could at least wipe his ass! . . . but never mind. It'll get better. I can't wait until I find someone truly sexually mature.

"If a double-decker bus kills the both of us,

to die by your side is such a heavenly way to die."

19 September, middle of the night

Fuck if I know what time it is. Past midnight. I'm at the art table at the studio at Squirrell in Portland on the planet Earth on one end of a spiral arm in the Milky Way Galaxy, all of that macro-existence reduced to a circle of white in an ocean of black, silence except for the rare sound of cars on the street outside. I let the tape player lapse because I was drawing straight lines and I couldn't stop even for a second, then I forgot that my world wasn't always silence. I just put on *Mysterio* and Ian McCulloch is wondering aloud if it's really such a magical world. Of course, the answer is no. That's the whole reason why I do comics. I see magic happen, and it slips through my fingers, but sometimes I can almost capture it on the page. Take Lise this morning for example—she leapt, flew, down the front steps, legs held out in a crazy ballet pose, something she shouldn't be able to do. But she did. And it was breathtaking. A *grande jeté* in combat boots. I want to freeze moments like this in life, the way I can in a panel. Sneakers aloft. Hair in perfect golden-tipped spikes, as distinct as weapons. Her dark eyes lifted heavenwards, her throat hurling forth a deep sweet note. "La!" On the bus stop she confessed that she'd had a little too much coffee, and that she was still high on the orgasm she'd had last night. Why can't I keep this moment? Not in my memories; I mean *really* keep it? Can I freeze time at these moments and treasure them until they lose their meaning, then move on to the next?

No, that's crazy talk. I need to get my head together and get back to this panel before I ruin it. I didn't even script this; I'm just drawing it, straight out of my head. Cabby stands with feet modestly turned together, gazes heavenward, curls and fumes of smoke or tripping-trails swirling around him, foaming into liquid waves at his feet. At his mouth is a small word bubble; in the bubble is infinitesimal lettering.

"I understand"

"Squire, remember, your review's at three today, so I'll take your calls," said Beth as I dragged my sorry self into work on the twentieth.

". . . What? Oh—shit!" I was wearing one of Lise's stripy T-shirts, a bit stretched out in the chest, and the usual jeans, which were dirty. My gray sneakers now had a hole in the rubber toe. "Oh, no. Oh, great. This is just great."

"You had three weeks' notice to prepare for this," Beth snapped impatiently. "It's too late to stress about it now. Besides, you should know how it's going to go."

"Do I?" I sighed. "Do I, now?" I put my face in my hands.

19 September, 10:12 a.m.

Shit. Review today after lunch. And I look like a skank and I probably smell like pussy. Wouldn't it be nice if the smell of my sexual prowess would intimidate the freaky ass morons who run this world and they'd get out of my way and let me and my lady live our lives?

Maybe I can have a massive stroke before three.

1:15 p.m.

At the bar. I ordered a Long Island iced tea and a side of chips and guac. I'm feeling a little more clearheaded as I eat, drink, and smoke. Sheeezuz Christ. I was literally shaking all morning and I just sat on the phone, pretending to take calls when I was actually just listening to hold music and nodding and saying "uh huh" whenever Beth or anybody else in charge walked by.

I hate life sometimes. I really do. This is ruining a perfectly good day. It's not too hot, I got a little sleep, we had a lovely shag first thing in the morning AND I got to work on time, my hair actually looks kind of good (I washed it, conditioned it, and then Lise dragged me down into bed before it was dry—so I've got perfect fashionable bed-head) and . . . oh, who am I kidding. I should finish my grub and get back up there. I think I want to have a wank first—it should relax me a little bit, maybe help me keep my head together against the slings and arrows I'm bound to face. Uuuughghghgbllfth.

4:14 p.m.

In the bathroom. Shaking all over. I wish I was a girl, so I could cry and feel justified. Maybe I should take a Robert Bly course so that I could reclaim my inner wimp and burst into fat, cleansing tears on a moment's notice. I weep, but it just comes out as thin, bitter tears that smell like tobacco smoke.

I know Trace knows I'm in here, and I just don't care anymore. Let the Nazis come into my attic and whisk me away to their ovens and their experimentation tables; I give up. I want to go home and . . . but where is that? Is Lise's place my home now? Or is it the room in Mom's Bellingham apartment above the bookstore? Or that shitty, tiny back bedroom in the duplex in Ballard, or something before that? Have I got anything in this world? Have I ever?

Of course I do. I have this journal. I have the hands to write with, and the pen, and the ink, and the propellant thoughts. That is all I can ever count on. Well, there's Lise. She's just downstairs. I want to sneak out the window and climb down over the bricks and snatch her away from Pronto and then we'll go sit on the concrete steps in the warehouse district and smoke and she'll smile at me and tell me I'm pretty. I'm sure I'm not very pretty right now.

Fuck this whole situation. I don't know how I'm going to get through three more hours of this idiotic charade, "performing" a task that I hate, for people with whom my mutual loathing runs deep. I just want to flee.

When I went back to my desk everyone became silent. I sank mechanically down into my chair, slid my headset on, and took the next incoming call, making no attempt to speak in any way than a dead monotone. It was preferable to screaming, or sobbing, or spitting, or grabbing my headset, and my phone, and my computer, and hurling them eleven stories down onto the street below. I imagined that action in great detail, and it played in a loop in my mind for the rest of the day.

That night, Lise and I lay together in the grass in the cemetery. It was a moonless night and we both wore all black, so that we couldn't be seen. Lise hugged me tighter still. "I'm sorry, baby," she said again. "It's okay. I've got you."

"No—I mean—I'm fine now." The tears had run out. I was empty. A dead, empty void, lacking anger, will, malice, fear, or concern. A perfect employee.

"At least they didn't fire you," she murmured.

"No." I shrugged. "I don't understand it. Apparently I haven't done anything right in months. I guess all those calls I answered correctly don't count for shit when it's coming from me because I am such a horrible person. It's not like they couldn't get some other know-nothing dumbfuck to fill my chair. Folks are lined up around the block wanting to work for the legendary Link-Up Telecommunications." Fresh rage swelled out of the nothingness. I had an endless supply, a self-renewing resource.

"They won't let you go because they know you're brilliant," she rationalized. "You *are* a good tech. You know this shit. And they know you're stressed, and you're not doing this just to piss them off."

"Doing what?" I snapped.

Lise blinked at me, big astonished eyes. "You know you can be a little difficult. You're just too smart and you're so far ahead of them, but they're just . . . y'know." She sighed and kissed me on the nose. "They think you're fucking with them. They think you're trying to piss them off."

"But I am," I protested. "I'm pissed off. I hate that place. I hate the work. I *hate* them. I'm a piece of shit and I want them to hate themselves as much as . . ."

She had her hand down my sweatpants (well, her sweatpants, but I was in them) and she began to gently, insistently stroke my penis. I lost my train of thought. All the blood in my body rushed gloriously downward to my groin and settled in my cock, making it achingly hard and turgid in seconds. Lise smiled without looking at me, and edged the waistband of the sweats down, exposing my penis, my black pubic hairs glistening in spider-web curls in the light coming from the street. I could hear cars passing by on Stark Street, the rumble of fruit trucks in the warehouse district. I gazed up at the trees overhead and listened to the sound of her sucking me, gently, trying to be discreet and firm at the same time. Oh, we'd been promising ourselves this for days. I tried to get into it.

She raised her head and we looked into each other's eyes, and both our hands met on my prick and stroked it off. I didn't hold myself back this time, and within less than a minute I wrenched my tool painfully across and shot a silver strand of spunk against the concrete headstone in whose shade we'd hidden. Lise looked at it and smothered an explosion of giggles. "D'you think that's maybe good luck?" she grinned.

For some reason I didn't find it funny. I was overwhelmed with a dizzy sense of doom that required me to close my eyes and grip double handfuls of cemetery grass. In response to Lise, so she wouldn't see me freaking out, I sang a line from a Duran Duran song—"'The world spins so fast that I might fly off . . .'" Lise is a sucker for Duran Duran. It worked. She climbed on top of me and started wrestling me, teasing me that I was going to raise the dead. I turned my face away from her so that she wouldn't see my grimace, partly from the discomfort of having her on top of me, partly from the discomfort of having had a quick, painful, and dirty orgasm, and partly because of the spinning sickness of vertigo that turned rapidly into a splitting headache.

It was no good. I didn't deserve this.

25 September, 9:04 a.m.

@ Triste. I couldn't sleep all night. I even drank some wine and smoked a roach Lise left in the ashtray, but I spent the evening looking out the window at the Leatherworks sign, listening for the sound of cars going up Belmont Street so that they wouldn't startle me when they came into visual range. I couldn't wait to get out of the apartment and come down here. Lise is probably still asleep—she was really tired last night and she didn't want to have sex, or talk, or watch TV. She just came in and stripped down to her panties and pulled the quilt over herself. I stood there and watched her relax into sleep, envying her already.

I brought *Ocean Rain* for the Triste staff to play. There's a new waitress here who I hadn't met before—a pleasant hippie woman, thirty-ish, with a young toddler (a boy, I think) asleep in a car seat behind the counter. She saw me sitting on the sidewalk outside the café before she opened; she let me in fifteen minutes early and let me have a double shot for free. I sat here at one of the back tables away from the window and watched her take the chairs down, wipe down the tables, grind coffee. She put the tape on without giving me any shit about it, which was nice for a change. Nobody else who works here will let me anywhere near the stereo. The sound of it swells gorgeously like an erotic sensation, bigger than in the apartment, more profound, seeping all through me so that I'm twisting about on the chair in the back of the cafe, so fantastic. I love this whole album.

It is not mellowing me out, though. I'm not sure why. My heart is pounding for no reason, and I've barely had half my coffee. It was hammering away all night, really. Not like tachycardia, but like I'd been lifting weights.

I wish I'd been able to sleep. That's two nights in a row. Last night I didn't even try for more than a few minutes. This isn't good. I don't really operate well when I haven't slept. At least I'm not at Link-Up day or I'd be seriously screwed. There are yellow and green circles dancing around the periphery of my vision. When I press my fingertips against my closed eyelids, the bright spots last a long time. But I don't feel *bad*. My stomach aches, and my head aches, and I'm having trouble focusing my eyes, but I don't feel *bad*. I feel like I could run a marathon.

I can't believe there's a baby in here. He's awake now— definitely male, I can tell by his expression. Big, dark eyes. The waitress bends over him and she's talking to him, her flimsy dress tightening over her back, spine ridging, shoulder blades. Damn, she's a skinny hippie. In contrast her child is plump and very smooth, glowingly smooth, his expression bullying and malevolent. Already. He's a little tiny miniature Rob. And his mommy is just doting on him. He's a little Hitler, this bambino, with his buttercream cheeks and fairy lashes. This is my enemy. All things cute on the surface, and hateful and hostile underneath. While I, kind of twerpy and weak on the surface, contain within my mind all things that need to be known or experienced. When people hurt me, they don't seem to realize that they disrupt the universe. Within each person, there lies an individual cosmos. I, right now, am unable to process that any other cosmos exists, or at least, every other one ought to be exactly like mine. But obviously, it's not. People wouldn't attack me the way they do if they had even the tiniest ounce of compassion for someone else, any appreciation for the simultaneously precious and infinite cosmos held within.

Blah blah blahhh. . . What the FUCK was that? What am I talking about? See what happens when I don't get enough sleep? Carl Sagan takes over my shit. This is the kind of weak, over-intellectual nonsense that got me into trouble in the first place. This is the kind of blather that enrages the Robs, big and small, of the world. Makes them mad. Them. Against me. That's all there is to it.

Not a good belch. I think I'm going to be sick.

"You okay in there?" came the waitress's voice through the closed bathroom door.

I couldn't respond for a few seconds. The espresso had boiled off, and I was dry-heaving, the whiteness of the bowl echoing the impotence of my belly. Lyrics. Filtering through, filling in the empty spaces in my bones and giving me the necessary animation to speak.

"*I'm the yo-yo man always up and down,*" Mac sang, "*so take me to the end of your tether.*" Violins, not gentle or peaceful, but slashing like scalpels; I envisioned myself at the end of a noose, a violin bow slashing the rope, and I fell. I felt it so clearly that I felt my neck snap and the floor rushing up to me. But I never hit the ground. I just kept falling. I groaned, and slammed my forehead into the toilet seat; the sudden pain in my skull brought me back to reality.

"Hey? Dude?" the waitress called.

"I'm okay, I'm all right," I said faintly. "Just . . . need . . . Bunnymen . . ." My hands were shaking so badly I could barely work the flush handle. With the swirl of water, the blinding headache spread from my forehead to encompass the whole skull, my vision crowded with dancing circles of green and yellow.

25 September, 9 p.m.

I didn't go to the emergency room. It would just be too embarrassing to go past the car-crash victims and go up the counter and say "I can't sleep and I'm having blackouts." Sensibly, instead, I went to the store and got some generic headache-p.m. tablets. The weird thing is that I don't remember leaving Triste. And yet I don't not remember it. It is liminal. It hovers between seen and not seen.

However my Bunnymen tape was safe in my pocket so it's not all bad.

Lise brought home leftover sushi, but I'm not hungry. Despite my difficult morning, I'm horny as fuck. She is smiling at me from across the room. I think I'll go eat her sushi—I love me some lady sashimi—and take some more of those p.m. pills, because they don't seem to be working.

28 September, 2:30 p.m.

Slept most of the last two days. Needed it. Thank God. Feel better now. It was worth missing work. I don't remember calling in, but Lise says that she woke me up yesterday and made me do it. I also apparently fell asleep in the middle of fucking her, still hard. Proving that she is the best woman in the world, she isn't even mad at me. I will make it up to her.

I woke up this morning thinking about my father, which happens from time to time—not as much now as when I was little, and more than when I was an adolescent. Something about that threshold of genuine adulthood, post-twenty-two, when you know once and for all that there's no going back to the way it was. You're always going to be taller than knee-high (although, not much taller, in my case). You don't want strawberry ice cream first thing in the morning (and if you do want it, you tell yourself that such an idea is disgusting). The Smurfs lose their appeal, and you can only enjoy them in a half-satirical, half-wistful backpedaling kind of way.

My father was named Jeremy Rutledge Squire. The name always made me think I was the disconnected orphan cousin of some British royalty—nothing grandiose, just a marquis or earl—but Mom assured me that he was ordinary Cockney trash. Just prettier than most. My father gave me my middle name, Bronwynn, which was his paternal grandmother's name, because he'd hoped that I would be a girl. (I never had a chance, did I?)

Mom says I remind her of my father—again, less than she used to. I think it was obvious that it kind of bothered me. I have a couple of pictures of him when he was about my age; a rather effeminate gentleman, shoulder-length black hair and very pale blue eyes, never smiling, but rather straining his sleek head forward on a long, skinny neck as though perpetually posing for a *Vogue* cover shot. In one photo my mother had caught him outside the Beatles' Apple Boutique, the Paddington side, on the day the Beatles let everybody raid the place for free, and he's holding an inflatable spotted mushroom ottoman (that Mom still has, collapsed, in a cardboard box in the basement). The picture's in black and white, but I can imagine the amazing colors of his velvet and fringes and flares. The other one is he and my mother on holiday in Mexico—sunburned, freckles, wearing a white T-shirt and jeans and no shoes. It's in color, and he looks awkward, uncomfortable, and skinny. Next to him my mother is tanned, grinning, and incredibly pregnant with me. It was 1972 and she totally looked like the young Stevie Nicks, though she denies it up and down.

My dad committed suicide because of me. Mom hollowly assures me that it wasn't my fault—and I know it wasn't my "fault"—I did nothing, consciously anyway, to convince my father that the black void and being slowly eaten by dung beetle larva was better than another minute on this earthly plane—but I know pretty surely that it's my presence on this earth that drove my pa over the edge. He was more or less gay, Mom admits. She was his fag hag. Or maybe he was asexual, but they don't tend to have hags. She was enamored of him—she, one of the zillions of free-lovin' hippie chicks who flocked to England in the late sixties, hoping to ball a Beatle or shag a Stone, and he, this glamorous, beautiful antelope from Stepney who was too proud to admit that he wasn't really turned on by women—not really men either, actually. Married my Mom, much later managed to knock her up, and even managed to smile when I was produced. And, apparently, he really liked me once I was here. He didn't trust himself around me—he thought men had no place around babies, and never held me when I was little because he was afraid he might drop me. "He just never seemed like he was . . . there," Mom said once. "He was wonderful to me. We honestly loved each other. But he never seemed like he could concentrate on anything. I called him my 'fairy visitation' . . . he thought that was funny."

One day, when I was three, Mom just got fed up with his non-involvement; she made him take me to a playground and play with me, alone, without her (if they both took me out to play, my mom would end up doing all the work while my dad wrote in his Moleskine or stared off into space with his blank baby-blues). He didn't know what to do with me, so my mother suggested swings—

pretty simple, and she figured even my flaky-ass father couldn't fuck that up. What happened next is ambiguous—apparently, he was roughhousing with me on the swings, we were having a great time, he was pretending to be a bull and charging me, which made the swing twirl—and he accidentally knocked me off the swing into the sand, and I broke my collarbone and hit my head. They had to rush me to the accident and emergency ward. Unfortunately there had just been a dreadful car crash and they were full up, so I had to wait in the lobby for hours with my head in my father's lap, and he let me sleep. When I was finally seen, they discovered that I'd had a severe concussion and that sleeping was the worst thing I could have done, and I might well have died while waiting to be admitted.

I hate emergency rooms.

That next night, when Mom was visiting me at the hospital, my father locked himself in the garage, put the radio on, and kept the motor running. He was quite dead by the time Mom got home. She's only rarely hinted at how fucked up she was, with her child nearly dead in hospital and her husband blue and stiff in the garage. It must have been a very bad night. I asked her what she did, and she said, "I called my mom and asked her if I could move back home. Then I smoked a joint, drank a bottle of wine, and got some sleep. I knew I'd need it."

She never remarried, though she did have a selection of semi-sleazy boyfriends in the early eighties. At a rather young age, though, she swore off such nonsense and dedicated her life to the bookstore. She's pretty vibrant for a woman who, as far as I know, hasn't had sex in ten years. I don't know how she does it. Maybe when you get to that age, it just doesn't matter anymore.

Oh, no, how could I forget . . . there was that incredibly brief fling she had with, of all people, Lise's dad Alex. I think it was only one night—a week, max. And I don't know if they ever had sex. I never asked and Lise never asked. Mom and Alex both decided that it was too weird, since their kids were best friends, and the thought of forcing us to become family was just too repugnant for everyone involved.

I can't believe I forgot that. I've been nailing my almost-sister for weeks. And nailing her hard. I literally cannot even believe how fucked up I am. I really don't belong in this world.

Lise planned to meet Lucas and I for drinks at the bar down the street from the Squirrell Press offices. It was already ten, and Lise hadn't shown up yet, so Lucas and I just started drinking. We had a pitcher of margaritas and a brand-new carton of cigarettes, and our hands on the table were stained proudly with graphite and ink. "When are you planning on going home?" Lucas asked.

"I dunno . . . probably just go with Lise. But I might stay longer. I'm kind of amped." I lit a match and waved the phosphorus smell away. "I've been staying up really late recently. At first it was hard, but I'm kind of getting used to it. I'm able to do a lot more stuff."

"That's cool; like what?"

"Oh, keeping a journal, trying to write stories . . . sketching the street outside, so maybe I can go back to doing my own pencils." I noticed Lucas looking at me with dismay or incomprehension. "I mean, eventually, I'll be doing another book, and I'd like to do the next one by myself. And in the meantime, maybe Kaplan will give me a break."

"Uh . . ." Lucas took a big swallow of his margarita, and wiped salt off his stubble with the back of his hand. "Um, Kaplan just gave me a raise. I think he's thinking about letting me ink, and just keeping you for lettering, and finishing the book on the next issue. I don't think you're going to do another book at Squirrell."

"What?"

"I don't think it's quite fair what he's doing to you here," he mumbled. "I thought you should know."

"You think he's trying to get rid of me?"

"He just upped my page rate. Like, quite a bit."

"No shit," I sighed, and drained my glass.

"Take it easy, man, you could get another book easy. No problem. I mean, the story's kind of played out; the art's still good, but the story's like, ehhhh. There's nothing wrong with your inks, as far as I'm concerned. You're good. Kaplan's just a motherfucker."

"He's a motherfucker who's giving you more money than me," I said, wagging my finger at the bartender. "He's a motherfucker who's giving you your own title. He's a motherfucker who's on *your* motherfuckin' side." I arched my eyebrow at the bartender. "Get us another pitcher, please."

Lucas looked at me strangely. "Hey, man, I didn't do anything to . . . Dude, it's just business. I told you, I don't think it's fair."

"Damn straight it's not fucking fair. It's bullshit. It's more bending me over and making me take it like the asshole I am. Is that all I am to you guys? An asshole that you can ream whenever you're worried about the size of your dick?"

"What the fuck is wrong with you?" Lucas stood up and pushed back his bar stool, blood rushing to his face. I turned away from him. I just didn't give a damn. I deserved the beating. Let it come. But Lise arrived, sat down in Lucas's discarded bar stool, and stuck her chest out cutely. Showing *him* the tits that I figured were *mine*.

"Hey, guys, sorry I'm late," she cooed. Lucas relaxed behind her, grabbed a new stool for himself, and sat down beside her. "Whatcha talkin' about?"

Lucas's eyes didn't leave the pert swell of her chest, nicely exposed under her tight camouflage-patterned T-shirt. *Boom, boom.* She'd put on eyeliner and red lipstick, even. I looked at them both and said, "Nothing you'd be interested in. I don't feel like rehashing it; I just want to drink."

So we drank, and Lise and Lucas talked about *Star Wars* and the Beastie Boys, and I smiled and nodded at the appropriate pauses. I loved both of those subjects, but tonight, they were unimportant and annoying, the exact same thing that everybody talked about all the time. It was tiresome. I had real feelings, real experiences to talk about.

At around midnight, Lise and I got a taxi home. I spit on my hands, rubbed them together, and wiped the ink and pencil-lead off my hands onto my jeans. They really needed to be washed. I wasn't looking at Lise. She was too sexy and evil and I didn't trust her right then. She smelled delicious, the combination of the smell of the musk shampoo and patchouli lotion, sweat, girl pheromones, twining together into a witch's brew. "What's the matter, honeycakes?" she chirped, cheerful and tipsy.

"Work bullshit," I mumbled.

She hugged my arm. "You okay, Bronwynn?"

"Why do you ask."

"I don't know," she said. "You just seem so down all the time. I mean, I'm used to your moods. I've known you for how long? I know you're basically a gloom-meister . . . but for some reason it has a different quality now. I'm not the only one who's noticed."

"Who else?" I demanded.

She blinked. "Who? Well, shit, I mean, I dunno. Just folks. You seem mad a lot more these days. It's just weird. It's probably my imagination—if anyone's got a right to be pissed off, it's you."

"Yep," I agreed, and managed a laugh.

"Let's just go home and get high. I just got some really nice herb. It's happy pot."

"There's no such thing as happy pot. That's an illusion. Somebody told you it was happy pot, and you smoked it, and afterwards you felt happy. It's just metaprogramming."

She sighed a little and rolled her eyes. "Well, I don't care how I got that way; goddamn it, I'm happy. I've got a gorgeous boyfriend, I've got a great stash of weed, I just got paid, and damn it, I have a gorgeous boyfriend."

"Who? Tell me who it is, so I can go beat him up." Miraculously, my head and chest actually did feel lighter. The feel of her soft cheek against my forearm, the warm blast of air from her lungs, the crunchy-silk spikes of her hair—hard to think about how unjust my workplace was with that sensuous treat on my skin. I bent my head down and kissed her forehead.

"Michael Squire, when are you going to get it through your head that you are a beautiful boy? I mean . . . you think your father's a good looking fellow, don't you?"

"Well, yeah, he was."

"You look a lot like him. And your mom, a little bit. You have her mouth. You got the most beautiful features of both of your parents. I think your mother is beautiful. Just because you're not six-four and don't have, like, massive greasy Conan muscles doesn't mean you're not cute. Think Syd Barrett. Think Mick Jagger."

"Oh, God, no."

"The *young* Mick Jagger."

30 September, ten to midnight

At Squirrell. Taking a break from sketching. My heart's not in it. I can't keep myself together.

Thoughts which have consumed me today:

1) How much I hate this charade that I still have anything to do with this comic book. How I should just go do something on my own again and start from scratch. How Squirrell and Lucas and Cockblock Kaplan are strangling me and how I'm sick from lack of air. Why am I even still here?

2) How glad I am that Lise doesn't shave. There is little that's as pleasurable as rubbing my freshly shaved face (what I do shave, anyway—only the goatee and the neck and fine hair on my upper lip and the tufts that would be sideburns if I let them grow) against Lise's furry armpits and the delicate hairs on her legs. She thinks it's pervy, which turns her on. I want her. I should go home and make her horny.

3) My most peculiar childhood.

I don't consciously remember my father's death—I was far too young, and no human being is very good at remembering anything to do with intense physical pain—but it certainly affected me. My mom has told me about it enough times that it's taken on a holographic quality. But I do remember the emergency room. It's almost worse than really remembering it because it's only fragments interspersed with memories of being in so much pain and seeing my daddy so scared. And that's all I really remember of him.

My favorite things when I was a child were *Archie* comics, the largest possible boxes of crayons, yo-yos, and the medical section at the public library. I rapidly got sick of children's books (though I never did get over my obsession with Winnie the Pooh) and found all kinds of amusement in the 610s. My mother never really knew what I was reading—I only checked out and brought home books on art, Greek myth storybooks, and the like—and she encouraged me to go to the library as much as possible so she could have some time to herself (and her semi-sleazy boyfriends). When I was seven I came down with a crippling headache and a high fever; they rushed me to the hospital and administered tests, sure that I had meningitis. They found nothing the matter with me—I'd just been reading about meningitis and other related inflammations of membranes. After that I had a different hysterical illness about once a week, once every two weeks—I could wrench myself into fever in a matter of minutes; I broke out in spots, hives, rashes; my liver hurt, my spleen hurt, my heartbeat was irregular; I had false tonsillitis so many times my mother finally humored me, and let me have them surgically removed. After that, the hysterical sicknesses disappeared like so much bed-wetting.

I have to commend my mother; she dealt with all of this with aplomb, grace, and humor; I guess my dad prepared her for that. If I had a dollar for every time I got beat up in elementary, junior high, and high school, I'd be a wealthy man. I never bothered to bring lunch or lunch money; Mom just paid for all my school lunches at the beginning of the year, or I didn't bother to eat. She would, without comment, ice my black eyes, put cool washcloths on my Indian burns, wipe the blood off my chin, and then we'd go play skee-ball, walk along the train tracks, or see a film or an art exhibition. For a long time I just accepted my place in the world, in the pecking order, as the Victim. It's not that I wouldn't fight back—I always would. I would initiate fights, sometimes, indiscriminately, with boys, girls, the bullies, and the meek. I always wanted to know people's breaking points. It became something of an obsession when I was in eighth grade and nearly got me expelled, especially since I tried to bait the school principal into hitting me. He got a clue and instead skipped me a grade up to high school, thus complimenting my intellect and getting me the hell away from him at the same time. A superior tactitian, that Mr. Wise.

I can't sit still anymore.

On the evening of October first, after bailing out of Link-Up, I got coffee before heading to Squirrell. I wanted to be able to work like crazy that night, come up with some new ideas, maybe some new sketches to show to Cock Kaplan. I wasn't sleeping much anyway; I figured I might as well work. Maybe I could get a new book at the only publisher I'd ever known. It was the devil I knew.

The day had been chilly, the first really chilly day of fall, and I'd started wearing a ratty old cardigan over my worn T-shirts and jeans. Any pretenses of a "corporate image" were completely out the window—while all the other support techs at Link-Up had started wearing clean clothes, no logos, (sometimes the women even wore pantyhose), I clipped my overgrown hair out of my eyes with cheap plastic barrettes, and washed my clothes only when Lise did laundry. My hands were black and blue with ink stains. I liked it; my hands looked ancient and gnarled, as if I had stolen them from someone three times my age.

The Squirrell reception area was quiet and deserted. "Hello?" I called, going through the hallway to the studios and offices in the back. "Hey, Lucas?"

"Squire, come in here a minute," came Cock Kaplan's voice, disembodied, in the hall.

He and Lucas Listener were sitting in his office with shots of brown liquor in front of them on Kaplan's black lacquer desk. I always hated Kaplan's office—that kind of studied yuppie hipness, big framed Lichtenstein print, black lacquer, brushed steel.

"Sit down, Squire," said Kaplan. He edged a shot glass at me with his little finger and filled it brimful of Johnny Walker Red.

1 October, some fucking time

So that's it. That's just it. All there is to it.

My lifelong dream, crushed out as casually as I put out a cigarette. It's as if my degree, my experience, my refreshing line drawings, were just a joke, a lure to get me to lay my head upon the chopping block.

The worst part was that shitty little smile on Lucas's face while Kaplan dropped his bomb. I can't believe that shit. He knew all along. Why would he lie? Trying to protect my feelings? Bullshit. He's just the same as everyone else. He just wanted to soften me up so that Cockblocker could plunge the spear in deeper. I could just grind that smile off his face.

Whatever. I told them to shove it. Shove the whole publishing empire up their anal trenches. I might have knocked something over, or maybe just fantasized about it. Guess I'll just walk now. Wired on coffee and rage. Not a fucking chance of getting to sleep this night. I don't even want to sleep. I don't want comfort. I could go home and snuggle with Lise, get stoned, blah blah blah. It would just be postponing the inevitable, wasting my life some

more, as if my life is a valuable resource in the first place. No, it's a joke, a bad one, and nobody's laughing.

I'm actually scared. Scared enough to admit it.

That night, I walked home from Squirrell, listening to tapes on my Walkman. Only three miles or so, less than two hours, what with waiting for red lights. It wasn't as long as I wanted it to be, but it wore me out anyway. I cut through the cemetery and sang out loud as I went through, and by the time I got to the front gate, I felt better. Lise was already asleep when I got in. I didn't wake her. I drank what was left in the bottle of gin, lay beside her, and drifted off for an hour or two until it was time to get up and go to the other job.

I walked there, too. I didn't want to make any contact with another human being, even accidentally. I didn't want anybody to smile at me. I could pretend to be a singing ghost, tramping along the side streets and train tracks and bridges, an invisible chorus of English rhymes.

I should have been incredibly early—the sun was coming up on my walk—but I was four minutes late by the clock in the reception area. Hours had just slid by without my notice, and I was late again.

I went and sat at my desk, clocked in electronically, and stared at the call queue on my phone's readout. Five. I had to check my email first, though, just in case.

"Squire, could I see you in the hall for a minute?"

I looked over my shoulder at Beth. I didn't even have my headset on. I was staring blankly at an open e-mail window on my computer monitor, an e-mail from Juba, and I had no idea how long I'd been sitting there. "Sure," I said, and followed her out of the room into the hallway. She didn't have an office, just a cubicle with the rest of us. But she wasn't "the rest of us." She was middle management.

"You've barely even pretended to work today," she sighed. She folded her arms and looked at the floor.

I looked at the floor too. It was pretty boring. "Sorry," was all I could think of.

"What do you mean, 'sorry'? Squire. For Christ's sake, is there something you need to tell me? I mean, geez, what's the matter?"

"Nothing," I said.

"For one thing, there's not a dress code per se, but it is supposed to be 'business casual.' That means no jeans. And if they are, at least you can have them be clean."

"They're the cleanest pair I have right now," I said. "At least they're black, right?"

"You've gotten paid since you moved. You could have bought some clothes."

"With what time? I have—I *had*—a whole 'nother job." I winced. "Besides, I don't really like shopping. It makes me uncomfortable. Besides, what's it matter what I look like? I'm on the phone. My voice sounds perfectly professional."

She made an astonished, impatient sound. "Look. I'm not your mom; I'm not your therapist. I'm barely even your acquaintance anymore. But didn't we used to kind of be friends? At least a little? I don't want to come down hard on you, but I'm having a really hard time covering for your fuckups. Everyone else in the department is taking the calls that you won't do. You don't even pretend to care half the time. This is a business, Squire, not a preschool."

"I'm pretty sure I saw Dave eating paste earlier," I quipped.

"This isn't funny," Beth sighed. "Shape up. Now. Or else. This is a genuine chance to turn this shit around before it's too late. Take some fucking calls."

"Okay," I said. I wanted her off my back. Her voice made my head throb. "I have to go to the bathroom; is that all right?"

"You're not on drugs, are you? I mean, you can tell me if you are. We can get you some help—"

"No," I replied, waving as I walked down the hall to the men's room. "I don't take drugs anymore. They affect my clarity."

I went into a stall, enjoying the quiet, tracing the rough grout lining the wall's tiles with my fingertip, listening to the soothing music of the water pumps. When I got back to my desk, an hour had gone by. Nobody said anything. I put my headset on and grabbed a new pad of Post-Its. I don't remember any of the rest of that day or the next one; I didn't write anything down.

3 October, 2:18 a.m.

I can't sleep at night. C'mon and hold me tight.

It was a very bad evening. I must keep telling myself that it's a whole other day; it's now the third of the month; all that is behind me. I've been sick. I got the night out of my body, and replaced the taste of bile in my mouth with the chalky purity of toothpaste. Lise stood over me while I was being sick and rubbed my back, gently, repetitively. I sent her to bed, telling her I needed a shower. I took the shower and I feel a little better. No, that's a lie. I'll never feel better.

Lise and I went to Gentson's for some brandy. She tried to get me stoned first, but I didn't really feel like it. I'm glad now that I didn't. Lise looked wonderful. The black satin dress that makes her look like a jazz-age tap dancer; hair slicked and curling at the neck and temples; bright red lipstick. I wore some of her clothes— a black silk shirt and red pants of some kind. We looked pretty groovy and I managed to forget, for an hour or so, about what happened at work today with Beth, about Squirrell, about the ridiculous travesty my life has become. We sat at the bar and listened to piano music and felt ourselves very tasteful, elegant, and happy.

Then Lucas Listener and his girlfriend came in. She's a real looker in the classic sense—tall like Lucas, thin, graceful, with a horsey smile and blonde hair full of bounce, body, and sheen. I felt Lise get tense, and her smile calcified on her face. She turned back to the bar.

I couldn't take my eyes away, though. I stared the bastard down. He walked up to me and said "Hey, Squire. This is my girlfriend, Amanda." Of all the things she could be named, her name is Amanda. I said "Let me guess; you're twenty-three," and she squeaked something in the affirmative. Lise was muttering at me to stop right there, but I just couldn't. I felt a rush like I was on a rollercoaster. I finished my glass of bourbon and stood up to Lucas and told him to his face what a sneaky bastard I thought he was. So he punched me in the mouth. It wasn't very hard, I realize now—he could probably have pulped my face with those hands of his, huge and stone-hard from all his drawing. It still hurt, though. Startling. I didn't fall down. I just shook my head and then calmly sat on the bar stool again. I ordered another glass of brandy. They wouldn't give it to me; in fact, they kicked Lise and me out. So we stood in the cold, waiting for a bus for half an hour, shivering in our cute going-out clothes. Lise didn't talk to me while we were waiting, but on the bus, she put her arms around me and kissed my hair. She told me she loved me. I wanted to cry, but I couldn't. I can't now. I want to do something. can't even do nothing. I'm just hanging on, wondering when it's time to scream.

6 October, 11:14 a.m.

To the logical limit.

So that's it, part deux.

I'm free.

And I have to admit, it feels good. At last I can finally do what I fucking want. Right now I'm on the bus going back home, where I am going to get high and go back to sleep.

I got the shaft from Link-Up. Oh, I guess I should be heading to the unemployment office, but guess what? I have plenty of time!!! And it's not like I'm going to get unemployment. Fired with cause. *Really serious* cause. Oh, fuck the world.

Trace did it himself. I came in, on time, jeans freshly washed, hair slicked back with gel from my eyes, ready to get to work. Slept last night and everything, even if it took the last six of the PMs in the bottle. My desk was cleared, all my stuff in a box (mug, pens, postcards, Rubik's Cube) on top. The Post-It gallery was just gone. I stood there staring at it, and then Trace emerged from the hall and said, "Squire. My office. Now."

Cold, cold water all over me, I could feel it soaking in. Adrenaline. My brain becoming sharp.

He made me sit down, and told me flatly that I was immediately "terminated" (I envisioned an enraged Schwarznegger pumping me full of lead) and that I was to take my stuff and leave the premises immediately. He slapped a paycheck envelope on the desk. "What's the cause, if there is one?" I asked reasonably, downright pleasantly.

"Your collection of online photos," he said. "Your child pornography. It's lucky we don't turn you in to the police. 'Cept that it's obvious that a fuckup like you isn't producing the shit; you're just enjoying it."

"The girls?" I asked, catching on. "Oh, no, you don't understand—they send those to me all the time. I never asked them for it. I'm not getting off on it; it's artistic. It's an aesthetic thing. It's nothing. It's a just a silly Internet thing. They're comics fans. They don't turn me *on*. They're in high school."

"Oh, I *know*. And don't try to justify it to me. I don't want to know. I just think it's sick and it's stupid. And we want you out of here."

"Is that the royal 'we'?" I said, and I got up and got my shit. I walked downstairs with my heart singing. Oh well, there goes my Internet account. Like I care. Like the Internet didn't lose its appeal for me as soon as I was employed there. It's just like the rest of the world. It's another cosmos inside this one, *of* it, not separate from it—it's just as stupid, just less ugly, most of the time.

But fuck, what about Lise's birthday? Oh, shit.

Time to ding.

I came into the apartment and took off my nice clean jeans, my cardigan, and my T-shirt, and crawled back into Lise's bed. I thought to myself, firing up the half-smoked bowl still in the pipe, that I should have gone into Pronto and told Lise about being fired, but it was too late now. Outside it began to drizzle. Perfect. I fell into a peaceful, blissful, calm, undrugged sleep for the first time in ages.

". . . What are you doing here? Squire, are you sick?"

Lise was shaking me. It was dark outside. I blinked at her. "Uh, no, no, I was just taking a nap," I mumbled.

She hadn't changed out of her yellow work shirt. She didn't take it off now. She sat in the chair opposite the bed and lit a cigarette, and began unlacing her boots. "I was gonna run to the store," she said, exhaling. "You want to come?"

"Uh, no, not really."

"You want anything?"

"I got fired," I said.

She blinked at me, put her cigarette down, and kept unlacing her boots. "Why?"

"They um . . ." I'd never told her about Juba. It really just didn't seem relevant. The pictures honestly didn't turn me on, but . . . they were so intimate. I never told anybody about them. They were just dumb kids having fun with being transgressive. And yet I'd never told anybody. There was no way out of this; I had been doomed before I even began. I felt the cold water trickling over me again, but this time, I felt like crying. "They just . . ."

"C'mon. You're coming to the store with me. Get up; put your clothes on. Put on a sweater; it's kind of cold out there."

Together we walked out of the warm, dim cocoon of the apartment into the dark, cold, rainy courtyard, and onto the street with its noise of cars. The disorientation was severe. She walked a few paces ahead of me, on the way to the store, then turned and faced me. "So what're you gonna do now?" she asked. She took my hand.

I took a deep breath. "Take it easy for a little while," I said, sighing it all out. "Relax. Think about what next. Get my resume together."

"Good idea," she said.

"I paid rent, at least."

"That you did." She squeezed my hand.

"And I have plenty for next month, as long as I don't spend my whole paycheck on clothes."

"Oh, just spend a little of it. You need a new pair of pants; I didn't want to say anything, but I am really sick of black jeans. And you could use a new sweater."

I felt so much better. I kissed her. "Let's get a really good dinner tonight," I said. "I'll cook."

I made her filet of sole in brown butter and toasted crumpets with marmalade, and we had vanilla ice cream with Kahlua for dessert. And then we took the bottle of Kahlua into the bathroom with us and had a very long, hot bath together. We didn't speak. We only needed the warm waves of understanding lapping against our skins for an hour or so. We went to bed early and we didn't have sex, just lay together, gently falling asleep.

For the first few days of my unemployment, times were great. I slept in, took my time, made espresso drinks, watched TV, cooked myself and Lise lovely suppers, and sketched my new ideas. A new character was taking form—a superhero, a self-parody, almost. I had been drawing Cabby for so many years, it was hard not to draw him; but every time I saw those round blank eyes and that psychedelic soft-serve swirl of hair, I would simply deface the drawing and see what came out. I showed my new sketches to Lise, but she wouldn't really respond to it; she seemed preoccupied. I didn't care. I was in a free-floating haze of pleasure. The journal has nothing from these days, but I remember them because they were so nice, the same way I remember the details of a week spent in England when I was eight years old. Some good memories just stick.

One weekday, the week afterward, I really wanted a sandwich from the bar downstairs from Link-Up. I don't know why. Pure perversity, perhaps, or the force of habit. hard to retrain the taste buds. I was downtown anyway, at Art Store, browsing for new papers, and I figured that nobody would be there, as it was a little early for lunch. I got my usual place at the back of the place and held up the menu as a signal to the wait staff.

The front door opened and Moll Malone walked in, her hair frosted with the thick mist outside. I thought about hiding behind the menu, but I just stared at her, and she walked over and sat down. I wanted to warn her that her back was to the door, that it wasn't safe for her to sit there, but I couldn't speak. "Squire?" she asked softly, cautiously.

"Howdy," I said, setting my menu down.

"What are you doing here?"

"I was hungry," I said.

"It's a bar. Who goes to a bar to eat? Oh, wait, never mind." The waiter came. I ordered a falafel sandwich and a shot of gin. Moll got a Caesar salad and a Diet Pepsi. We looked at each other. "I miss you already," she admitted.

"Really? I thought everyone there hated me."

"Not everyone. Not me." She smiled.

"Yeah, but who does? I mean, how did they find those files? That was my computer."

"It's the company's computer."

"I didn't do anything wrong," I insisted. "I never asked for that stuff. They sent them to me. Nobody was hurt. For Christ's sake, they're just teenage girls with a fucking digital camera."

"You should have thrown them away," Moll mumbled.

I shook my head. "I told her to stop sending them."

"You could have set her address to bounce."

I grimaced. "We're . . . I kind of . . . we're kind of friends now," I mumbled. "She wants to study art in college, too, so I kind of counseled her . . ."

Moll sighed. "What I think is really sick is . . ."

"What? What do you think is *really sick*, Molly Malone?" I snapped.

The waiter brought our drinks.

Moll was swallowing hard. I sipped my gin, regret almost making me gag. "Randy and Dave were messing around with your computer while you weren't there," she said, defiantly. "They went through all your files. E-mails, too. They printed them out and showed them to Trace; showed him your computer. All while you weren't here. And I'm sure they were looking for nudie pictures. They've got plenty of their own saved on their own hard drives. Just that yours are better."

I smirked. "That's why I didn't throw them away. She's just a kid, but she's a really good photographer. I told her to study Man Ray and then get back to me."

She smirked too.

We clinked glasses.

"I'm thinking of quitting, myself," she sighed. "I can't take much more of this shit. I'm really sick of Randy and Dave. I'm sick of Trace. I think I might go back to school; become a vet."

I told her she'd be good at that. We ate and talked about inconsequential things. I did not talk about myself, or what I'd be doing next, because I didn't know and I didn't want to fuck it up by conjecturing about it. When we were done, we exchanged phone numbers and promised to keep in touch. As soon as I was on the street, I dropped her business card into the first wastebasket I saw and watched it get soaked by a thickening rain. It would be better if she cut off all association with me.

The Mighty 10-10, 12:43 p.m.

Lise's birthday. Hooray! She's in the shower. I'm making coffee. We're going to the movies and then we're going for a drink at the Rolling Pin. I feel shitty about it, but I really almost don't care that it's Lise's birthday. I'm just so not in the mood to be festive and attentive. I got up early this morning—too early—and just doodled. Total useless doodling. Pages and pages of text—lettering—as though I were studying for a typesetting class. But it was just letters, just the alphabet, Lorem ipsum and the Quick Brown Fox. But I can't seem to stop writing today. It hurts not to. It hurts my *brain*.

2:30 p.m.

Bathroom, Broadway theater. I just don't care about this movie. Lise has wanted to see it for a long time, but I can't remember why; she's just sitting there, beside me, barely breathing, almost dead. I can remember the commercials for this movie, but I don't know who's in it—certainly not Tim Roth or Isabella Rossellini, that's for sure. Clean, sculpted Hollywood types in this one. Complicated, possibly romantic plot. I could give a rat's ass. I hate romance.

Someone has scratched into the paint in the stall, "I suck cock." There's something about that that's touching to me. No phone number, no forwarding address, just that defiant, bold statement. It was the only release the poor fucker had. He'd never admitted that to anyone before. Or maybe he didn't; he just wanted to. I make art for people like that. Those people with something horrible and unspeakable inside that they can't confess to anyone, ever, but will kill them if they don't get it out somehow. That's how I make art.

7:18 p.m.

FUCKFUCKFUCKFUCK. Fuck. Eff. Blah.

Well, that about tears it, doesn't it?

Lise just had to "pop by Pronto to see how things were going," on her day off of all things—how we Americans worship the

94

workplace!—and she just happened to step over the threshold into a huge "SURPRISE!" and balloons and a cake and party favors and all that gagging rot. And she fell for it like a redwood. "No way!" and "You guys rock!" and "I had no fucking idea!" which makes me want to fucking puke, since she wouldn't be flipping out if indeed she had known—so she *did* want to go to Pronto just to see "how things were going." How sick is that? Who is this person? What's the matter with this picture?! And then when I don't seem thrilled, she tells me that we can go drink at the Rolling Pin anytime, but this was her birthday, and nobody had ever surprised her before, and if I needed to, I could just go home and she wouldn't mind and she wouldn't take it personally. And I looked around at all those shining Pronto faces and I showed them all my teeth and went out and got back on the bus. I can't believe how much my life sucks right now. I can't even believe it.

On the other hand, *of course*. You're a piece of shit, Michael Squire, and *you know this*. Everybody knows this.

I'm eating a previously frozen national brand "pizza" and watching *Jeopardy!* on my girlfriend's birthday while she parties down with a bunch of husky boys with callused hands and does the Cabbage Patch to the Spice Girls with her manager. I might as well go to sleep soon, and if I'm lucky, I'll stay that way.

11 October, 5:10 p.m.

Raining outside, still. It started last night and has kept up pouring hard ever since. The gutters are choked with wet leaves and flooding, creating reservoirs of black water that each car carves into a voluptuous wake. In the yellow light of the Leatherworks sign it looks like an arc of fire in the dusk. At least it does right now.

I had a terrible dream this morning that shook the hell out of me. I lay there stunned for a long time after I woke up, wondering how my own mind could betray me like that. But I've thought it through, and I am now prepared to give an analysis.

In the dream, I was on a skateboard, which I haven't done since I was an adolescent jerkoff (like so many kids, I was a snotty rebel, unable to admit that I craved acceptance, and would throw away my *Megadeth: Kill 'Em All* T-shirt forever just to be able to go to the middle school dance). I wore big, shiny, new Air Jordans with super-thick, untied laces and floppy tongues; shoes that I wanted when I was that age, but never acquired in real life. I was skating down Hawthorne in the middle of the day, but there was nobody else around, no people and no cars.

At the corner of 39th and Hawthorne, I paused for a stoplight (Why? There was nobody else in sight—stupid). Suddenly there were a couple of cars that drove by way too fast. They crashed into each other with a big sound of crashing glass and screaming metal—it sounds like a cheesy exaggeration, but how other way to describe it? It was like a woman's scream, like a thousand bottles being smashed at once. I've relived this in nightmares again and again since I was little. There is almost no way to imagine the brutal orchestra of sound it creates—it's easy to see why J.G. Ballard thought about it as highly sexual . . . It'd be so intense to a benumbed populace, right? The memory has never been sexualized for me—for me it's far more primal—the animal, mammal, sense of pure adrenaline. Some jock would probably think it was fun. That shit isn't fun.

So the cars crash into each other and people are flung from the cars, etc., into the street. Suddenly I'm surrounded by people, the way 39th and Hawthorne usually is, and everyone's looking at the wreckage skidding to a halt in front of the Washington Mutual bank. I find myself skating up to the wreckage, determined to turn my rush of adrenaline into energy to help people. Of course in real life I'm not really able to do this. Few people are. Once in a while I am actually useful in a crisis—I once got into a fight with the school bully and knocked out one of his front teeth, and I was the one who picked up the tooth and rushed it to the school nurse so that they could put it back in. That guy never picked on me again.

There was a middle-aged woman lying on the road with her skull cracked open. I got closer, steeling myself against the gruesome sights, but instead of blood and brains, her smashed head was oozing this weird beige gooey stuff. Only upon closer inspection did I discover it was oatmeal.

"Oatmeal?" I said out loud. Nice smelling oatmeal, too, with cinnamon and maple. I started to laugh. On the other side of the car a little girl was badly mashed by a car door, but she smelled really good, and I started getting hungry. When I went even closer, wondering if I should taste the oatmeal, I saw that none of the people involved in the accident were real, but instead they were highly realistic mannequins or something, made out of something that looked kind of like papier-mâché.

I turned around and skated home as fast as I could, and instead of the Barton Apartments on Belmont, it was my mother's place, complete with the bookstore on the ground level. I ran up through the apartment door into the house, and my mother was there, drinking tea and doing a crossword puzzle. I was so relieved to see her and see that she was alive and real that I hugged and kissed her and held her desperately for a minute. She couldn't figure out what the big idea was, so I explained to her what I'd just seen—the wreck, the oatmeal, all of it. She told me that it was just a nightmare and that it wasn't real, but she didn't laugh at me or tell me I was crazy or anything. She got up to put on more tea and then she slipped and fell down, hitting her head on the linoleum. I ran over to see if she was all right, but she was dead, her head broken open. Inside of it, she was full of ashes—fine ashes like cigarette ash, post-cremation ash. Now that she was dead, I could see that she was made out of papier-mâché, too.

I got furiously angry. What a cheat! I went out into the street and grabbed a shovel and started bashing in the heads of every person that came near me. All of them dropped and revealed their artificial nature. Everyone was like that. They were all made of paper and full of oatmeal and ashes. Every person on earth had been replaced by their exact duplicates, made out of waste products. I didn't know how I'd missed it, but none of them had been real all along. I was the only real one—or was I?

I ran back into the bathroom and began bashing my head against the tiles until I felt my skull begin to give way, and looked into the mirror to see if I was fake and full of oatmeal. Instead, my face was all bloody, and there was a big dent in the side of my head. I could see pale brains peeking through masses of black and bloody hair. At first I was delighted—I was real after all! Then I thought, *oooops, uh-oh, well . . . oops.* And now I was going to die. I was going to die any second.

Needless to say, I woke up at that point. It took me a long time to shake the feeling it gave me—I had to take a long hot bath, drink a pot of coffee, a couple of shots of whiskey, cigarettes lit butt to butt. Even now I'm petrified by it. I mean, it was so funny sometimes, and it made so much sense; it was so real that all of *this*—the Formica kitchen table, the black-and-white checkerboard tile, the yellow sign and the splash and whir as the cars go by outside—seems fake, like a billboard looks like a photograph until you're close to it. I've determined at this point that the dream's meaning was one of the following:

1) I'm going to commit suicide.

2) There are two distinct classes of people on the planet. They are divided into THEM and ME. Am I the actual mutant? Am I really as abnormal as I seem? They will win. There's no doubt about that. I can't take care of the whole world myself when I have only the power of one person. Is there any point in fighting an unwinnable battle? Why not just gently, gracefully, obligingly, lay down my sword and extend my hand in fealty?

3) It was an internal message from me to myself, about self-understanding, and thenceforth, developing greater understanding of others. I, of course, am flesh and blood. In the dream, I died for the emotional worth of that. I wanted to be human. Yet, every other being I saw around me was sham, a mock-up, hollow husks filled with the detritus of modern civilization—packaged oatmeal, cigarette ash, two sides of the same coin. I am the only one of my kind, and I just killed myself. Good work, stupid.

4) I'm losing my motherfucking mind.

Quit crying, pussy. Sleep is for the weak.

12 October 4:20 a.m.

Ha, ha, 4:20.

Ever get the feeling that your life is locked into a pattern, and nothing you can do is going to change that? I can't figure out if they want me to kill myself, or stay alive so that the humiliations can continue. Maybe it's just my suffering that's keeping the world even spinning, because I can't figure it out otherwise.

I don't think Lise is asleep right now. She's too tense. Her sweet, tender, curvaceous body is rigid under the quilt and her breathing is shallow and rapid. I wish she had been there, to protect me, although she probably would have gotten pounded too. All the same, I want someone else to suffer, I want some kind of kinship in this world. Something.

I never thought that Dave could be so violent—he seems too fat and good-natured to want to hurt someone so bad. Want to hurt *me* so bad. I just don't understand. Or I don't *want* to understand. It all makes a sick horrible kind of sense. This is my fate. This is why I was born. This is why. Everything makes a sick horrible kind of sense.

I can't see out of my left eye. It's an amazing color—bloody reds and purples and hints of blue. That was Randy's shot, actually. The first one. The second one got me in the jaw and I dropped like a bag of Legos. Dave picked me up and propped me against the wall and hammered blows into my midsection—chest, belly, belly. Then he kicked my legs out from under me. Laughed. "I've always wanted to do that," he said.

Randy laughed too. "You little shit," he said. He kicked me on the side the head. Not hard, but hard enough.

It was at the Caravan. I had gone to see Old Gold, who are leaving on a tour of Europe next week. I was drinking. Randy and Dave came in. I went up to them and told them that they were a couple of hypocritical fucks, and that while snitching season was in, I had some interesting information about the two of them that Trace would be very interested in. Randy said I didn't have the stones. I held up a quarter and quoted them Trace's home telephone number, told them I had nothing left to lose. Then Randy grabbed me, practically picked me up, and dragged me outside.

Man, that was a real interesting bus ride home. I missed the band, of course. On the bus stop, a five-minute wait while I swabbed blood from my nose and mouth with the tail of my new T-shirt and rubbed it on the sleeve of my new jacket. Now they're all crispy. Everyone on the bus stared at me in horror and disgust, and I almost didn't care. My head hurt so much that I thought I was just going to pass out, but I never quite did. Tears ran out of my bad eye and ran down into my nasal passages, stinging the hurt part inside and making my nose run with bloody snot, which I wiped onto the sleeve of my jacket. Neither T-shirt nor jacket is black; light green cotton and cheery blue canvas. The blood stained both black. Should have just bought black ones in the first place. I tried to read the little poems that they display on the inside walls of the buses, but I couldn't focus, and the light was flickering moth-inside madly. I couldn't close the window and I had to keep changing seats because they were all wet, even the ones that looked dry.

As soon as I got off the bus I puked on the sidewalk. It was mostly blood, but there was some whiskey and beer. What a waste of money.

Lise freaked when I got home. I couldn't really talk to her. I went straight into the bathroom, stripped off my bloody and torn new clothes, and took a long, hot shower, soaping up my body and rinsing it off, over and over. I brushed my teeth and used mouthwash. It didn't help; I could still taste and see blood. I think one of my teeth is fucked up.

I should just change my name to Mike Pukey. I've never thrown up in my life as much as I have in the last couple of months. *Je m'appelle Squire Puke*. The Earl of Hurl. El conquistador del Vomitos. His most Eminent God-King of Reverse Peristalsis. Grout boy. I can't ever get clean.

I am actually in the closet right now. It's the best closet. It's huge, in the style of closets of the apartments built in the twenties, almost half the size of the entire rest of the apartment. Lise actually doesn't keep a whole lot of stuff in it. Most of her clothes are in her bureau or, mostly, on the floor. I put my egg-carton foam on the floor of the closet, stacked her shoes neatly on the perimeter, brought in my Itty Bitty Book Light so I could see to write. I just have to narrate all of this. The more I write out, the calmer I feel. What I really need right now is a cigarette and some Bunnymen—early stuff—simpler, more primitive, more primal. Serious stuff. *Crocodiles*.

I will listen to *Crocodiles* and then I will sit at the window and look out of it at the rain and the yellow sign. I will try not to bother Lise. This isn't her dilemma; it's mine. Mine alone. The mighty doomed struggle of Grout Boy, world's greatest fuckup.

THREE: Mirror in the Bathroom.

16 October, 9:10 a.m.

I have a job interview today—working at Art Store. I scored an application from the cute goth girl, and the manager called me. I told him I had retail experience, which I do, from the bookstore, and that I knew pens, inks, paper, brushes, paint, the works. I just got my clothes from the dry cleaner and I'm having a cup of coffee at Triste. The nice hippie lady is working here again, asking after my health. Apparently my face looks a lot better now. She's got her stupid kid with her as usual. I like that kid less and less all the time—he looks way too wise and experienced for someone who doesn't even know how to read yet. He walks, though, all over the place. He's always coming up to me and then falling down and howling. I'm sure his mom thinks I'm trying to molest him. She ought to get a goddamn babysitter.

11:55 a.m.

Well, so much for that job. I don't know what I said, or maybe it was just my looks, but the manager's face fell as soon as I came in. I couldn't think of anything to say in response to their weird questions. "We'll be in touch," he said. Bastard. I could grind my polished shoe into his face. Fuck them and their art supplies I don't need anymore and their retail. Fuck them.

17 October 10:20 p.m.

Worked on resume all day at the library. Lot of other bums there. Came home, made dinner, and then Lise and I had really wonderful sex for a couple of hours, laughing and oral and double orgasms for us both. She went to sleep; I'm watching *Star Trek: The Next Generation* with the sound off, listening to Bunnymen on headphones. Heaven Up Here. "Over the Wall." It's a Barclay episode. I understand Barclay.

I hope I can get some sleep tonight. I wish I hadn't taken all those pills. Not that they do much good, anyway.

17 October, 10:12 a.m.

I hate life. Another job interview. This one with a temp agency. I said I'd die before being a temp again, but I have to try something. This blows. I have a headache and my Walkman batteries ran out right in the middle of "Lips Like Sugar." Oh, well. It just reminds me of Juba. She doesn't even know what happened. She's probably getting bounced mail now and she thinks I've abandoned her. No internet access at home, and I can't exactly ask Lise to try sending Juba an email from Pronto. I should have written down J's phone number when I had the chance; I could call her and tell her what happened. She'd feel so guilty, though. It's fucked. I don't even know her real name.

1:30 p.m.

I answered the questions of my character test honestly.

Have you ever taken drugs? Yes.

Have you ever taken drugs at work? Yes. Aspirin, idiots. I wouldn't waste good drugs on being at work! (I didn't say that, of course.)

Have you ever gotten angry at work? Yes.

Angry enough to hit someone? Gods above, yes. Though I didn't actually hit anyone. I spend every moment of my life in the workplace angry enough to hit someone.

Have you ever been accused of a crime? Not yet. Oh, no, wait, I have. Child pornography. Statutory eyeballs.

I think I have a migraine. It's like there's this red curtain in front of my eyes—red with green and yellow circles sliding across it. I'm in a bathroom stall at the mall. A relatively safe place. I need to calm down, to detox. Can rage be considered a controlled substance? Bitterness is a poison. At least it's fucking Friday.

Sincerely, el Conquistador de Yak-Yak.

18 October, 4:10 p.m.

Sleep, wank, smoke, wander, read want ads, do crossword. Back to sleep. Lise is at a bridal shower at Julianne's house. Hope she'll steal a bottle of something and bring it back home; I could use a drink.

19 October, 8:25 a.m.

Lise went to work. I tried to eat some cereal, but it sickened me. I think I'll go back to sleep. Fuck this.

20 October, 2:00 p.m.

What a waste of an entire week. Nothing happened. I slept. I read the want ads. I hated everything I saw. Lise is on her period and she doesn't want to have sex with me, even though I told her I didn't mind. I think going to that bridal shower and breathing in all that estrogen brought her menses on.

NextTech, Link-Up's competitors, seemed interested, but apparently they actually talked to Beth, and undoubtedly, Beth told them they shouldn't let me work for them. I didn't even get to go for the interview—they called me about fifteen minutes ago, waking me from my stupor, to tell me that the position was filled. I guess I'll see what's on TV.

Lise came home at around six. A videotape of *Friday the 13th* which I'd gotten from the library was playing, but I wasn't watching it. I was illustrating, in colored pencil, the green and yellow circles that I couldn't stop seeing; I drew them over pages of my sketchbook, over finished and half-finished sketches of the defaced and perverted Cabby. I'd already listened to all of my Bunnymen tapes, and I'd moved onto the Doors, since it was nearly the same thing, just not as pure.

"How'd it go?" Lise asked, shrugging off her coat. It made me nearly sick to see her, day after day, go through the exact same physical motions, standing in place, to work and back and to work, each day the same as the one before. It wasn't right. She deserved better.

"They dissed me," I replied.

She scowled. "Oh, Squire. That sucks! I'm sorry." It didn't seem genuine.

"How was your day," I asked in a dull voice.

"Guess what," she prefaced, then paused, her excitement visibly building. "I'm an assistant manager!"

"Great."

"Dude. I am so psyched. This is the easiest job in the world and I'm going to be making fourteen bucks an hour! Fourteen bucks! Can you fucking believe it? I think we should celebrate."

"I don't feel like celebrating," I said.

"Oh, come on, Squire. It'll cheer you up. It's on me. Besides, they're just job interviews. You might as well take it easy, enjoy your time off. I don't actually need your rent money right now. Just take care of yourself." She slid onto the chair next to me, wrapping her arms around me; she wasn't hugging me, but just holding me between her arms, the rough material of the Pronto Printing polo shirt chafing my neck. "I'm worried about you."

"I'm fine," I said. "I'm just kinda stressed out."

"Well, shit, you should be." Her hand went to my eye reflexively. "That looks a lot better now."

"It's fine," I said. "I put a steak on it," I added.

She didn't seem to get the joke. "Do you want to go out?"

"Let's go someplace where nobody knows me," I said. "Somewhere we've never been before."

I found that I couldn't really eat. We went over to Hawthorne for Chinese, which for some reason never quite works in Portland. I had to sit with my back to the door, and I kept looking over my shoulder every time I heard the door or felt a breeze. The waiter was all over our table, filling our water glasses every time they dropped an inch, asking us again and again if the food was okay. I didn't like his weird neck with the skin stretched over his Adam's apple and scraped bald, or his false concern of whether we were "doing okay," and eventually I snapped and told him us to leave us alone. Lise spent the whole incident staring at her plate like it was some kind of magical transport device to get her away. "You're acting like a cokehead, Squire," Lise muttered. "Just cut it out. It's not funny."

"I'm not . . . trying to be funny. I'm not trying to be anything," I tried to explain. "I just . . . I don't wanna . . . I'm not that hungry."

"Damn it, boy, I finally get something to go right in my life, and you can't even be happy for me. You are the most selfish person I've ever met."

"I *am* happy for you," I protested, trying to smile. It felt like I was opening my mouth for a dentist's drill. "I'm thrilled. I just can't figure out why this means so much to you . . . I mean, it's just a job, right?"

"It's not just a job. It's fourteen dollars an hour. It's a shitload of money. I'm happy about this, Squire. I've been so broke for so long. It feels good to know that I can put hard work into something, and get something out."

"I wouldn't know; I can't," I said.

"It's not your fault. You were working in two brutal, shitty industries. They chew people up and spit them out again. I just got lucky. You've got to stop torturing yourself like this." She crossed her chopsticks on her plate and ran her hand over her hair, which was getting rather long, only the very tips blonde now, the rest a soft thick pelt of mink-brown. "I love you, baby," she added. "I hate to see you unhappy."

I hated being called baby. "I'm always unhappy," I muttered. "I was born unhappy."

"Oh, Christ, back to that again." She sighed. "Never mind, okay? Let's just go home."

At home she poured herself a stiff glass of whiskey and rolled a fat joint. "Have a drink," she urged.

"I don't want to drink anymore," I said, gently shuffling things around the closet. "It makes me sick. Maybe I'm allergic."

"Smoke some herb, then. That'll stop you puking."

"I might have to drug test," I said.

She didn't light the joint. "Shit."

"I'm sorry. You can maybe . . . smoke it outside? I don't know . . ."

We slept with our backs to one another.

25 October, sometime

There are those of us who are losers because we were
excluded from polite society, and there are losers who chose to be
outside from the get-go. Then there are people like me, the rarest,
who at an early age decided to be extraordinary, and then too late
had a change of heart and wanted to be like the regular kids. Of
course we failed miserably at that and made idiots of ourselves.
Somehow that hurts more than just having been a fuckup from
the beginning; we feel as though we brought our loserdom upon
ourselves, with our hubris ("I am extraordinary") or our foolish
choices ("Why shouldn't I go to the prom or run for homecoming
king? Everybody's eligible, right?"). The one thing that a public
high school adolescence teaches us is that whether we regret our
choices or not, there they are; I'm a geek, and I'll be a geek until
age erases our differences and makes toothless old idiots out of all
of us. That, more than anything, is the one thought that keeps me
from suicide—if I kill myself now, I die a geek, whereas Mike
Hunter the captain of the football team will also get broken down,
glaucomatous, and senile, and then I can laugh at him.

"What's the matter, Squire?" came Lise's voice through the closed
bathroom door.

I was in the bathtub, looking down at the wet smooth trail of hair
that led from my belly button into my pubes, my penis small and relaxed
and floating on the surface of the water. My journal lay on a towel beside
the tub; drops of water blistered the surface of the paper. I'd been in the
tub since it was light outside, and now it was dark and I heard prime-time
television starting up outside.

"My head," I replied pleasantly. "It's as though millions of voices
were crying out in pain, and then suddenly stopped."

"I have to pee. Can I come in?"

"Sure," I said, and dropped a face towel over my crotch.

Lise came in. I thought to myself that if she was wearing that yellow polo shirt again, I was going to scream, but she was, and I groaned instead of screaming. She dropped her corduroy pants and seated herself on the toilet. "You okay?" she asked.

"Yeah, great," I said.

The sound of her urine stream echoed around the bathroom. "Sorry I'm home so late," she sighed. "We had an emergency staff meeting. The bigwigs from Berkeley are coming next week, and we have to get the shop looking perfect or they're going to be doing some firing. It's yucky."

"What time is it?" I asked.

"It's a quarter to nine."

I grimaced. My hands were a mass of pruny wrinkles, and my cuticles peeled off like so much wet tissue paper. "Oh, crap, it's freezing in here." I lifted myself out, weak as a kitten, and wrapped up in a towel. The water I'd been immersed in had gone cold long ago. Lise stood up and flushed, then grabbed another towel and dried my hair. It felt nice.

"You don't look so good. Did you eat today?" She rubbed with the towel on my arms and back, tracing her fingertip over the Krazy Kat tattoo on my back. I'd forgotten I had it; I got it when I was eighteen, giddy and reckless with post-adolescent freedom.

"I didn't, really," I said. "I slept. And wrote."

"Oh. I was gonna get a pizza." She hustled me out of the bathroom and picked up the phone. "What do you want on it?"

"Make me one with everything." Quivering with cold, I put on my new set of red thermals, matching top and bottom, wrapped up in the blanket, and lay in bed. I hoped that Lise would notice that I was poorly, but she was smoking, watching TV, flipping through her mail. I gave up on compassion and shuffled to the kitchen, where I put a pot of coffee on.

"You're making coffee? At this time of night?" Lise asked quizzically.

"I'm cold, and I'm sleepy," I justified.

"You're making a whole pot? Why not have some tea? You're going to be amped up all night. No wonder you don't sleep."

Ironic. I sometimes slept for ten, twelve, fourteen hours at a time. Just not every day. Not most days. "I won't bother you," I said. "I think I'll actually get some drawing done tonight."

"Would you get me a beer out of the fridge?"

I handed her a beer. "Why do you drink every single night?" I asked her.

She gave me a very cold look. "Because I have a job," she said, and sipped.

Nothing to say to that. I sank down behind the partition, mummified in the blankets, and waited quietly for my coffee to brew. Lise made some impatient noises, then picked up the phone and called for a pizza with garlic, onions, olives, and feta cheese—the "Breath Freshener." I got the first cup before all the coffee had run through the filter, added sugar, and crept into the closet. The pen in my grasp steadied me, even if my hand shook. I could get the thoughts out of me so I wouldn't speak.

I don't know what the hell is up with Lise. She's been workin' for the Man for too long. She's not said anything hostile like that to me in a long time. I wish I didn't deserve this, but I'm basically an egotistical asshole, just like she said.

I'm watching her through the gap between her long dresses. She's finally taken off that loathsome fucking shirt. Underneath she's wearing a Hanes Y-front of the kind that we call "wife beaters." Horrible term. Her fat, dark nipples are lusciously outlined and erect—the apartment's cold. I'm afraid to turn the heat on, since I'm not paying any bills. She's toying with the nipples, circling them with her fingertip, her face leaning into the phone. What a goddamn shame. She doesn't touch herself that way when she knows I'm looking. She doesn't want me to see her naked, and I don't want her to see me naked. It's just the end of a beautiful friendship, a beautiful relationship, and I want to run out there and tell her that I love her so much, that she's the only thing keeping me sane, that I wish I could drip through her, a filtered colloid with tiny particles of Lise suspended in me—but she'd only cut me down, laugh at me, smack me in the face. I'm such an asshole.

She's on the phone again, more relaxed this time, laughing. She lights a doob. "Yeah, I'm smoking pot," she admits to the phone, and laughs some more. Obviously not the cops. Why does she have the TV on if she's not watching it? Is she ever going to turn the heat on? I want to do it myself, but I'm in the closet now. I wish she'd stop talking on the phone about pot. The police have ways of listening in on phone conversations—line taps, cellular things, satellite dishes. They're going to come in here and haul me off to jail.

Oh. *Shit*. She's on the phone with my *mom*. She said my mom's name—Marion—I know Lise doesn't have any friends our age who are named Marion. I can't quite figure out what they're talking about—Lise seems to be talking about work, regurgitating the same information as she gave me when I was in the bathtub. I wish to God she wouldn't talk to my mom, because I know she's telling Mom all about what I've been like, about how I've lost my jobs, blah blah blah. I haven't told Mom, and she hasn't called to talk to me, but I know subconsciously that she knows what's been going on here.

Lise nervously glances at me in the closet. I'm going to close the door a little bit so I can shut out the insistent noise of the television, blaring ads, strobing off the white walls of the apartment. I see Lise's apartment, and I want to paint it black, I really do. At least it's dark in here, except for the book light. I'm almost done with this notebook, and I need to get a new one. I thought it would last me for the year, but it seems seventy pages aren't really enough, not for my pen to glean this teeming brain. I write too big and I think too small. This is all filled with nonsense. Page after page of incoherent, immature scribbling. No wonder I lost *Cabby*. I am a sinkhole, a black hole, a singularity of suck.

Maybe I ought to just throw this away.

I shut the journal and slid it underneath the egg-carton foam. When I came out of the closet, Lise said quickly, "I gotta go," and hung up the phone. "Pizza's here," she explained to me, looking over her shoulder. I went to the kitchen to refill my coffee cup.

I was up like a shot in that grey, dry morning, shaken awake by a nightmare so formless and horrible that I couldn't remember anything about it except the sickening dread. I'd slept in my clothes. I was out of cigarettes. I went downstairs to the store across the street on the corner and put my last five dollars on the counter. "Can I have a pack of Winstons, please?" I asked.

"ID?" The Asian woman behind the counter was reading a tabloid and didn't look up.

"For Chrissake, I come in here every day and buy cigarettes. It's my goddamn birthday and I'm twenty-four. You mentioned it yesterday!"

"We're on camera," she said, again not looking up. "I don't card you, manager sees tape, I get fired. I know it's your birthday and I know how old you are, but the videotape doesn't know. I have to see ID every time. It's the law."

I fumbled in my back pocket for my wallet, but it wasn't there. I might have taken it out in my sleep because it was digging into my back. "I don't have it on me," I begged. "I'm dying for a cigarette. Can I grab these, and I'll go back upstairs and get my wallet, okay?"

Her smooth brown hand slid the cigarettes off the counter and flicked my useless currency back at me. "Sorry; no ID, can't sell. Come back with it."

"Shit." I trudged back across the street.

No keys, either. My temples began to throb with the first horrible rush of a nicotine-withdrawal frenzy. I felt like my bones had turned into ash. My jaw clenched; I wanted to urinate; chills went up my spine. And I thought, *Happy birthday, man.*

The apartment building's gate stared at me forbiddingly, its wrought-iron curlicues twisting into a menacing frown, eyebrows drawn down. Locked. You shall not pass. Keys. No keys. Fuck! I patted myself down, pulled all my pockets inside out, then sat down on the concrete stoop and listened to my breath shudder in and out. I needed the nicotine. I needed it. It was ten in the morning, I'd had three hours of sleep (I'd fallen asleep on the end of the futon in front of the TV, watching the repeat of World News Now become Good Morning America), and my lungs were imploding.

I decided to go to Triste and see if anyone there had a cigarette I could bum.

I didn't have my jacket, either, and the biting west wind had picked up since I left the apartment, slicing through my Primus T-shirt as if it were gauze. It was nineteen blocks to Triste. I walked as fast as I could, but my lungs would not cooperate, and I had to pause twice, gasping for breath.

The hippie lady was there, finishing pulling an espresso for a terse businessman. "Do you have a cigarette?" I begged her.

She smiled at me. "Hi, there," she said softly. "No, I had to quit when the nipper was in me. I haven't smoked since. Sorry."

My eyes started to tear up, but the businessman spoke. "I have one," he said, voice arch with contempt, though I'd just asked him for a laxative.

"May I please, please, please have one? I'll give you a quarter for it, if you want."

"No, don't bother," he sighed, and gave me a long, slim brown cigarette. I watched him leave the café, wondering if he were gay (what straight man ever smoked a More?), and wondering if I'd just outed him in the most oblique way possible.

"Need a light?" asked the hippie waitress, smiling.

"No, thanks," I said. "I have matches."

"You want to get a coffee?"

"Depth charge," I said. "Double. God bless you." I gave her the five dollars, and went outside to smoke.

That was one of the best smokes I'd ever had. The cigarette itself wasn't the very best, but I've never loved nicotine more than when it was coming from that slim, breakable cylinder. So what if it made me look like a fruitcake? That was nothing new, after all. I leaned against the brick wall of the Cafe Trieste, smiling and nodding at passersby. When I went back inside, I felt relaxed for the first time that day. *Happy birthday, man*, I thought, *for real this time. You're on top of the world.*

The hippie had only charged me a dollar for the depth charge, so I tipped her a dollar and went back to my usual table in the back. For a change, I wasn't the only patron; a couple of other hippies were in there, slumped in their fuzzy Sherpa sweaters and sandals and layers of flannel and faded calico. They were doing a crossword puzzle with the intense concentration of the stoned. My hands itched to write, and ideas hammered at my skull from inside. I couldn't bear to see the hippies with their pens, working together, murmuring, diligently filling in squares, when I was so helpless, bound and tied in my own thoughts the way I was, with no way to exorcise them. I was sick of being helpless. I went up to the counter, where the hippie barista was feeding her toddler from a small bag of animal crackers. "Excuse me, I'm sorry. Do you have a pen and some paper?" I asked.

"Oh, yeah, sure I do." She rummaged under the counter, and handed me five sheets of wide-ruled loose-leaf and a green ballpoint. "I hope you don't mind wide rule," she apologized with a grin. "I know it drives me crazy."

"If it gets on my nerves, I always just divide the lines in half," I said, and sat down.

They were playing The Doors' *Best Of.* "The End." I knew the track listing and the production of each song by heart. I consider the Doors to be Bunnymen methadone. I'd been listening to it a lot lately, trying to break out of my rut. But it, and the coffee in my mouth, seemed intensely bitter today, metallic on my palate.

I put the pen to the paper.

27 October

My birthday. I'm 24. Nothing.

lost in a roman wilderness of pain.

all the children are insane.

Jim, ya givin' me a migraine

and I'm never listening to the Doors again.

I am *hating* this. I bet the hippies had something to do with it. Amanda likes the Doors. That cunt. I wish I didn't harbor so much bitterness toward her, but I do. She's ruined me for any other person. Anything that reminds me of Amanda makes me want to shoot people. I think I have a lot of repressed anger towards her, always did; violent feelings that I suppressed, that I sublimated into lust, which is why I came all over her. I substituted spunk for the blood that I wanted to see pouring from wounds in her belly and chest. I used to rub my hand in it, playing with it, fascinated with its texture and its smell, which sickened her because she too could see what I really wanted. I wanted to gut her and then sketch her disorganized entrails. While listening to the Doors. It's the right soundtrack to a sick sex murder, which is why so many people like it—they have their own sex murder scenarios that play themselves out in their subconscious. Then they sublimate it and it oozes out as hostility towards me.

Fuck all of you. Go listen to the Doors and live out your sick little fantasies. I wish I had sex-murdered Amanda, especially after that last date. I could see her jeans disappearing into the crack of

her ass and I wanted to rip them off and fuck her hard on the concession stand, scattering popcorn and jujubes hither and thither. And then she opened her big mouth and I wanted my head to explode. That would have been worth their entertainment dollar—how often do you get to see a head explode in real life? But, of course, I couldn't do that. Like everything else, I didn't get it right.

I don't know what's up. But this coffee sucks. Whatever, thanks for the discount, hippie chick, but you can't make coffee worth shit. You could have pissed in a cup and put food coloring in it and it would have been the same. This place sucks, all their food and drink and "atmosphere," all bullshit and it always has been and they just want to rape the real patrons. The real people. Playing the fucking Doors on a weekday morning, as if it didn't make everyone go into a psychosexual rage. Don't they have any idea? That bitch snatch manager smells like pogey bait, and her stupid boyfriend Chopper sucks off little boys at the playground, and then jizzes in the sandwiches. I'd like to see *his* head explode. That and that coconut skull of that stupid baby, who's spitting up half-chewed crackers right now, trying to get me to puke. And *LAUGHING*!!! That little shit is laughing at me! Yeah, eat me, you little scumbag—your mother is a crackwhore and your father is a subhuman doper. Fuck off, all of you.

Fuck

Right

Off.

I punctured a hole through the sheet of wide-rule. I was shaking too badly to hold the pen, which had been slipping out of my fingers and making the last three sentences take forever. I ran my hand over my head and found my scalp dripping with sweat. I rushed to the bathroom with my hand over my mouth, bent over the toilet bowl, and made the coffee come up. It made me feel cleaner.

When I went back to the counter, I felt like I was trying to walk through a closet full of heavy winter coats. The "nipper" threw a half-chewed animal cracker at me. "Can I get change for the phone?" I asked, staring at the baby.

"Sure, man." The hippie chick gave me four quarters. "You okay?"

"It's my birthday," I said, and retreated into the phone booth.

It sure was nice in there. Though it smelled like stale air, ozone, and cheap cleaning products, at least it was away from the rest of the café, filtering the Doors enough so that I could almost forget they were playing. I felt sick, but I didn't want to throw up anymore. I gripped the smooth rounded edges of the telephone, willing my stomach to calm. Using the green pen I still held in my sweaty hand, I quickly sketched Cabby on the white paint of the inside of the booth. The effortless execution amazed me, so I did it again, and another time, each better than the last. But they looked too much like Lucas's version of Cabby, with the oval head and the slouch—not the round head and the rumpled shorts—so I scribbled them away until the ink ran dry. I dialed Lise's number at work, and as it rang, slipped both arms and my head and the phone receiver inside my thermal shirt. Inside it was as warm and red as the womb, full of my own comfortable sweat smell.

"Pronto Printing, Lise Ballard speaking. How might I help you today?"

I sat there for a second, not recognizing her voice.

"Hello? Hello? Can you hear me?"

"Lise?" I croaked.

"Squire, is that you?"

"Yeah, um . . . I locked myself out of the apartment."

"You what? Oh, Jesus H. Christ."

"I'm so, so sorry," I said.

"I am really busy right now, Squire. I mean really busy. Do you think you can chill until I get off work?"

"I really don't want to, Lise, I'm sorry. I really want to go home. I'm puking—"

"You're always puking. You're fucking bulimic. Look, I'm sorry, but you'll have to wait until my lunch break, at least. The Berkeley group is here and I'm supposed to have lunch with them. And I've got two people out sick today. Where are you."

"At Triste," I mumbled.

"I'll be there at noon," she snapped. "Don't move a muscle. And then I'm letting you in, and I'm going off to do lunch. Don't ruin this for me, Squire."

"Okay, okay, okay. I didn't do this on purpose."

"I really wonder sometimes," she said, hanging up.

I held the dead receiver inside my shirt for a while, listening to the dial tone roaring in my ear. If I could have died instantly, I would have. I settled instead for slamming my forehead against the wall next to the phone, hoping something would splinter.

That didn't happen, either. I staggered out, out of the phone booth, out of the café, back out onto the street, searching for someone walking by with cigarettes. In the time that I'd been on the phone, the street had become deserted. It had begun to drizzle tiny bits of ice which stung my neck and face like hot match heads. I sat down on the curb and held out my hands to it, my hands slowly filling with cold water. I could never catch and retain a single fleck of ice; they melted instantly upon contact with my skin. I went back into Triste, sat down, and slumped against the wall, sick and boneless. They had put the Doors album on again, starting at the beginning. Break on through. I couldn't.

At twelve-forty, the door flew back on its hinges with a dismaying rattle of the bell, and Lise marched in. "C'mon, Squire," she grumbled. "Let's go." She grabbed me by the arm and yanked me up from the chair.

She stomped along the sidewalk in her polished, thick black boots, corduroy trousers swishing, and let go, shaking me out into the gutter. "What the fuck is the matter with you?" she finally shrieked.

"Nothing," I moaned.

She kept walking, shaking her head.

I tried to explain. "I just went out. I couldn't sleep, and I needed some cigarettes, and I just left the house without anything because I thought I'd be right back. I didn't do it on purpose. I don't mean to bug you; I just don't know what's happening to me. And the coffee was so bad. And like, the *Doors*? I mean, shit, y'know? And I didn't have my ID, so I couldn't get cigarettes, so could you give me one of yours?"

"You have to be either high or stupid. And I don't think you're high. Damn it." She dug out her pack, almost full, and handed me the whole thing. "Give me one."

When we got to the apartment, she unlocked the front gate, the door, and the apartment door, and grunted, "If you can't handle going outside, stay home." She clomped back down the stairs and away.

After I had smoked and ate some food, I sat at the window and stared numbly down at the street. I saw the mailman approach. Desperate for anything to do, I skipped down to the first floor lobby to pick up the mail.

In the time that it took me to get down there, the mailman had been joined by a UPS delivery man. They both turned to me and examined me, my ink-stained and cartooned jeans, my threadbare t-shirt, my bare feet. "Apartment 218?" said the UPS man.

A stab of panic threatened to stop my heart. "H-h-how did you know that?" I stammered, backing away. I felt the cold-water shock again.

"I've seen you before," he chuckled, and handed me a big brown package. "Sign here."

I signed his proffered clipboard. The mailman handed me a thick sheaf of envelopes, then hefted a large box from where it rested beside him on the floor. "It's your lucky day," he said.

"It's my birthday," I mumbled, escaping before they could say anything else.

I took the mail upstairs and looked over it. All of it was for Lise. All of it. Along with the usual bills and circulars were dozens of envelopes filled with free samples of laundry detergent, eye shadow, paper, address stickers, tea. The big box had a return address from some company I'd never heard of. With an X-acto knife, I carefully slit the paper around the box. It contained multiple videotapes, variously labeled. MuscleFlex System™. Jaunty Grill™. Modern Office Solutions. Teaching English In Korea. 15 Minute Glutes. I vaguely remember seeing late-night TV ads for all these product offers, but they had only been background detritus spacing out acts of *CHiPs* and *Bosom Buddies* reruns while Lise and I passed the bong back and forth and traded kisses and handjobs. The memory turned me on, and I masturbated.

Afterwards I lay on my belly on the futon in front of the TV and went through Lise's stacks of unmarked videotapes. I'd always assumed they were videos that her father had made and sent to her; she paid no attention to them, and the tapes we actually watched were right on top. In reality, these mystery tapes were three- to twenty-minute promotional tapes for every conceivable product: CPR instructional videos, anti-drug propaganda, religious splinter groups, foreign-language company training films. They solidly filled the TV shelf back to front; behind the TV shelf were four banker's boxes full. There were enough of them to stack around myself, brick-wise, making a corral six videotapes high.

I curled up in my corral, careful not to knock against the delicate walls. It was almost cozy; a sarcophagus of advertising media. They all wanted to make me a better person. After a brief rest, I climbed out of the corral and sat on the floor beside it, smoking more and drinking the last of the coffee. I sorted the mail, then arranged it by color and size around and inside the videotape corral. Still, the composition was unbalanced, so I put some of the opened mail from the kitchen table in. A large empty space of hardwood floor remained in the center. I stared at it for a long time, gnawing my nails and smoking. I got up and grabbed random, small, colorful things from the kitchen table and the bathroom counter, arranged them in the center, two Xs and three straight lines. That made sense. I felt calm.

I ate a bowl of cereal, had another cigarette, took a long shower, crawled into the closet, and fell asleep.

The next thing I knew, I was being shaken. "Squire, wake up." I opened my eyes. Lise stood over me, the skin around her mouth white. "What is this? What . . . were you doing?"

"I brought you the mail," I said, rolling over and going back to sleep.

Halloween, 10:15 p.m.

Lise has gone to a Halloween party thrown by some people she works with. She asked me half-heartedly if I wanted to go, and seemed satisfied and relieved when I said no.

Outside there are some kids trick-or-treating, swaying down the street in ridiculous plastic costumes, led by Mommy (invariably Mommy), invariably dressed as a pointy-hatted witch. I want to go join them, in my costume of the Normal American Youth, get some candy for my trouble. I have such a very good costume. I have THC in my fat cells, rendering me unhirable for any lucrative job and liable for arrest on drug charges; I have uncombed, greasy hair; I have the flannel shirt, I even have the tattoo. I am a typical young man. I am a psychotic killer, a genius, a sex maniac, an imbecile, a world traveler, an artist, an alien. I don't belong here and I can never leave.

I've put *Crocodiles* on and the low soft throbbing that introduces "Going Up" hums through the apartment at a discreet volume. Then the drums pick up and it's like I've just cracked a

Whip-it, the rush of euphoria, the first slice of reverb guitar and the heavy velvet of Mac's voice.

Art thou watching my film, analysing me?

Damn, I love it. Practically swallowed, not at all like his later enunciation. Appropriate. A good beginning, ambiguity. They are after Mac, too, and he's garbling his words so that only he and Bunnymen fans can understand them. He knows what to do in times of crisis.

Oh, God, Mac, please be watching my film. Please help me figure this out. You're so beautiful; you can do anything.

I've drawing all evening doing a new comic. I think I finally have something:

The Adventures of Neurotransmitter Boy, Superhero of the 90s!

His green mask conceals his identity from the normal world. His costume is somewhat reminiscent of the typical Boy Wonder garb, but crossed with jockey's silks—he's a little fellow and the yellow and green circles on a background of red make him stand out so he can attract, then wallop the evildoers. Neurotransmitter Boy's powers concern the ability to control his own brain chemistry and that of others. With a single sweep of his cape, he can drive a den of gangsters into a dog-pile of dopamine dozers; he can distract his foe by flooding him with beta-endorphin, then flit off while the baddie writhes in ecstasy on the floor! Neurotransmitter Boy is practically invincible against anyone who isn't heavily medicated! And he never need feel chemically unbalanced. If he's bored, he can just have his neurons fire at random, giving him a free, legal, and harmless psychedelic "trip"!

A color sketch of Neurotransmitter Boy is taped onto the margin, flying in classic superguy pose, fist thrust toward the future. It's pretty good, but rough.

Page one:

Panel 1: NB flying through a gorgeous cumulus sky.

NB: Hurrah! My three-day weekend is here at last!

Panel 2: birds-eye view of a typical crosswalk. A Bully is walking across, though the signal plainly reads DON'T WALK.

Bully: Man, jaywalking is the best! Fuck that "look both ways" bullshit!

Panel 3: N.B., shooting downward.

NB: Crap, it's an evildoer! Better go interfere . . .

Panel 4: the crosswalk. N.B. swoops down and lands on the street, arms akimbo, safely out of traffic. The Bully continues on blithely.

Page Two:

Panel 1: N.B. is grimacing as he sends waves of energy at the bully.

NB: (thought balloon) I'll slow him down with some *pure melatonin*! Re-uptake *this*, buddy!

Panel 2: The Bully, in the middle of the crosswalk, gets a drowsy smile on his face. Birds circle his head.

Panel 3: The Bully gets hit by a VW bus full of hippies. N.B. is nonplussed.

NB: Another job well done by Neurotransmitter Boy! Now! The weekend! where's my crack dealer?

This journal is full and done. I should really burn it. Maybe it'll take me with it.

Days later I woke to the sound of Lise laughing. I opened my eyes and looked at her for a while, listened to her giving her name and address to someone on the phone. She glanced over and noticed me awake, and she slammed the phone down in a panic.

"Who were you talking to?" I asked.

"Nobody," she said lightly.

I closed my eyes again.

"Do you want to go to Triste?" Lise asked, nudging me with her toe. "It looks like it's stopped raining. I wouldn't mind getting a white chocolate mocha. Mmm, doesn't that sound good? White chocolate mocha, Squire . . ."

"Okay," I said. "Sure, that sounds all right."

"Get up and take a shower," she said. She was bright, perky, clean, dressed in a clingy sweater, a short felt skirt, and thick, fuzzy purple tights. Her hair was long enough to use barrettes again and she had three in a row on the top of her head. She looked really good, like she hadn't in a long time. "And shave. You're starting to look like a redneck."

I took a shower, and I shaved upper lip, under lip, one cheek, the other. The beard growth seemed even thinner than usual, but I was surprised at how much there was; I couldn't remember the last time I'd shaved. Probably my last day of work at Link-Up, weeks ago. I smoothed my hair back and wiped the mirror, looking at myself in it. My cheekbones and nose looked knife-sharp. My hair had grown long enough to cover my entire face in the front, and almost to my shoulders in back. My eyes looked huge in my thin face, the whites of them chased with swollen capillaries, the skin around them baggy and stained with fatigue. But I wasn't fatigued. I felt great.

It had indeed stopped raining, and the gutters surged with water and leaves and trash. Lise and I held hands as we walked along, avoiding the puddles. She said, "Call your mom."

"Oh, I will. I just haven't felt like talking to her. I don't know. There's certain stuff you can tell your mom, and certain stuff you can't."

"I wouldn't know, really," she said faintly.

"Sure you would," I insisted. "I mean, you can talk to your dad, right?"

"Uh, no, I can't, Squire. He wouldn't really care to know. He might say he cares, but he doesn't. I don't have real parents."

"I've only got one," I said.

"It's better than none."

I didn't want to remind her, again, that both her parents were still alive; it really didn't help when neither of them really wanted anything to do with her. "You can have my mom," I said, and laughed. "Really. Why don't you just take up where I left off? I think she really wanted a girl."

"Squire, that's not true."

"Bullshit it's not true. I mean, look at me. I'm a swish. And I'm not even lucky enough to actually be gay. She likes you better than she ever liked me."

"I'm Marion's friend," Lise said. "I'm her buddy. You're her kid. She likes me, but she loves you. And she likes you. I mean, shit, she likes you more than I've almost ever seen a parent like her kid. She was so cool to you when you were a teenager, when my dad was trying to put me in reform school. Marion came through for me as a friend. Your mom loves you, and she thinks you're cool."

I didn't say anything.

"Stop feeling so fucking sorry for yourself," Lise said under her breath. "You've got it pretty good." Then she kissed me on the cheek. "Mmm, smooth. You're not a swish. No swish can give me head like you can." That made me smile, and even though I could have kept arguing with her, that was a good place to stop.

We arrived at Triste, and I went in ahead of her, scouting for my usual table. It was occupied with some rocker guy and girl, obviously hung over, swirling their straws in their smoothies. I stood there looking at them, wondering if I should ask them to move.

Lise went up to the counter. "Can I get two white chocolate mochas?" she asked cheerfully.

"No."

Lise and I looked up at the same time. The manager was working her fantasy shift, Saturday afternoon, tip paradise, and she had on a tight flimsy top so that the guys would give her more money. "Huh? Why not?" Lise asked.

"Are you with *him*?" The manager pointed at me.

Lise arched her eyebrow. "Yeah, I'm with him."

"Then you don't get anything. We have the right to refuse service to anyone. I'm refusing service to that little fuckwad, right there."

"What?" I said, starting to laugh.

"You know what you did," said the manager, spit spray leaping from her mouth.

"No, I don't, actually."

"Amanda," called the manager. "Would you like to explain to your friend here why he's 86ed from here?"

The skinny hippie waitress came out of the back room, laden with her little boy, who was asleep against her collarbone. She held the three sheets of loose-leaf I'd written on in her other hand. Her face was stony, cold, and hurt. "Thanks a lot," she hissed. "I'm glad I was nice enough to lend you the paper."

I took the pages back and looked at them. "Oh . . ." I said in agony. "Oh, crap."

"Your name's not Amanda by any chance?" Lise, cringing, asked the hippie barista.

"Yeah; what difference does it make?"

"Shit," said Lise softly. "It's a long story. He's—he's—I mean, it's a long story."

"Just go. Now," said the manager, glaring at me, shaking her head slowly. "And don't come back, or I call the cops. That goes for you too, sweetheart."

"What did I do?" Lise whined.

"You obviously made a grievous error in judgment," said Amanda the hippie lady, and went back to the back room. The child woke up just before they went into the back; he opened his eyes, looked directly at me, and smiled.

We left Triste, and walked back up the street, heading to Spoons n' Cups, a café we almost never went to. It had halfway decent coffee that nonetheless never tasted quite right (the espresso was okay), and more soupy/salady things than Triste did. We didn't really talk. Lise just looked at me with a very odd expression on her face. "Can I read it?" she blurted, reaching for the pages.

"Don't touch it," I said, snatching it away. I folded the pages and stuffed them in my jeans. "It's—very—private."

I kept the pages there, next to my skin, not even trusting my pockets, all day. Later, after Lise was asleep, I tucked the loose pages into the back of the journal I'd just finished, and put it on the top shelf of the closet. I have no idea why they didn't just get thrown away, but if the writing's survived that fate twice, it might as well stand.

FOUR: I'll Show You the Life of the Mind.

The second diary is a blue hard-backed lab booklet with yellow, narrow-ruled pages, its cover thickly covered in red, yellow, and black electrical tape in a kaleidoscopic mandala pattern. It's really quite beautiful and I don't know exactly how I did it. The strips of tape have been applied such that only the barest slivers of the original cover's blue vinyl show through, but just enough to provide a shimmering three-dimensional pattern. The tape makes it heavier than the other. It's an object. In the intervening time, I have never dared to open it again, superstitiously afraid that the ideas will get out. But I'm doing it now. The sun's still out, if only for a little while longer.

5 November, midnight

is this the blues I'm singing?

Happy V for Vendetta Day.

I don't go to Art Store anymore, and I couldn't find the right kind of notebook. I knew the one I should have. It came to me a few nights ago. I saw it with my mind's eye, and I couldn't get back to sleep. I lay there and faked sleep and listened instead to Lise making phone call after phone call. Sometimes she spoke, sometimes she simply began punching number keys again after a few seconds, and I could tell by the pattern of her tapping that she was hanging up, then dialling another number. It was eleven taps, plus one very soft one at the beginning. Long distance. Or, more likely, 1-800 numbers.

I hear her do this in the evenings before I wake up. I hear the the television, an ad, one-eight-hundred fill-in-the-blank. And then her fingers will start caressing the phone, as she used to caress me. And then the dialing begins again. As soon as I show signs of life, she hangs up and pretends to be cleaning her nails or packing a bowl of dope.

Oh, I miss her. I miss our life together. I miss the midnight cunnilingus, I miss the baths and the lying in bed too small and too warm for two, I miss the way she used to look at me first thing in the morning, as if I was too good to be true. She's a million miles away. But she's right there, six feet away, face down, the quilt covering up all of her except her feet. I wonder if she's faking it. I should close the door.

It's like a private room inside the apartment. I've moved Lise's shoes into a box just outside the door, and swept the dresses aside so I can have room enough to sit up straight, with my back to the wall, knees slightly bent. I can curl up and sleep here. I've supplemented the egg-carton foam with a pillow I bought on the same day as I bought this notebook, and a *Star Wars* sheet. The closet holds warmth admirably.

Lise is asleep in front of the TV again. I watch too much TV now that I'm unemployed. God knows what kind of electromagnetic radiation Lise absorbs while she sleeps—I must, too, actually, since I'm usually still asleep when Lise comes home, and she invariably turns on the TV so she can catch the news. She watches the news now. It sickens me. I want to scream to her "What are you doing?!? You're sucking up what kind of falsified information, what variety of whitewashed propaganda, what kind of lies that your mother and father and MY mother struggled to help you transcend?!?!?" But she'd only look at me like I'm crazy. Once someone is lost, you might as well just deal with it and get on with life.

Hey, look, it's a Link-Up commercial! Such lies. Such deplorable lies. "It's easy!" It's not easy if you've got porridge for brains, which seems to be the case for ninety percent of the customer base. "It's fun!" Until you see your bills. "It's the future!" The future happens whether you're looking at alt.fetish.wet-and-messy or not. They might as well take the simple route and say, "Having an account at Link-Up will either get you hot chicks, or pictures of hot chicks. Either way, your dick's not big enough." People think I'm kidding.

124

Now the TV is showing an EyePlace ad. I need to go there to get my eyes checked. They called around all over town until they found me here, to "remind" me about an appointment. I never told them where I lived now; I never gave them this number. Yeah, my glasses are being held together with duct tape, and I have to squint one eye to see stuff at a distance, but I'll get my eyes checked when I'm good and ready. I'm not going to go just because I saw an ad on TV.

A soda sounds pretty good right now. No, wait, what am I saying? I don't want soda. It's cold in here and I'm full of coffee. I can't handle the electronic hypnosis. Somebody needs to go night-night. —— Better. Now it's dark but for the street light, and my book light, and silent except for the sound of my exhales.

God, what a rough night. It went like this:

Lise came home, and I was awake, in the bathroom in front the mirror. Lise came in and peed like I wasn't even there, then left like I wasn't even there. She poured herself a shot of whiskey and opened a Mickey's bigmouth, then lit up the rest of the bowl she'd started the night before. She smoked and drank in front of the TV, then made herself a bowl of couscous and raisins. I stood in the bathroom for a while longer, watching all this happen in the mirror. Then I went into the kitchen and looked into the fridge, but everything in it looked like cardboard and death. I settled in my chair by the window and looked outside. Lise came over and stood by me and asked "Do you want to have sex?" And I said "What?" and she said "Never mind." And then I asked "Do *you* want to have sex?" And she said "Yeah," and I said "Um, okay, but just a second," and I turned down the TV and put *Heaven Up Here* on. And we started kind of making out. I felt terrible, like my body was made of rubber, like I was watching Lise do it with a sex doll, like I wasn't even a part of what was going on. And then she tore away from me and sat up and said "Can we at least listen to something other than the Bunnymen?" and I said "No, we can't." And she said, "Never mind, Squire, I changed my mind, just do whatever you were doing." So I went back to the bathroom and looked at the mirror, watching her stop the tape and turn the TV back up. I wish I knew what just happened there, but I don't. I wasn't really there. What's the matter with making love to the Bunnymen? We used to do it kind of often. Well, once. And it was great. I was floating in a sea of liquid pleasure then, fingers and slippery cunt and condoms and Mac's voice, Mac's words, Mac's understanding. *Whatever burns burns eternally, so take me in turns, internally. When I'm on fire my body will be forever yours, nocturnal me.* Why doesn't she understand. She is not the same Lise.

I miss her.

6 November 4:15 p.m.

I just woke up.

In my dream, my mother was dying of a crushed larynx, we'd been in a car accident, and she was bleeding to death while I begged passersby on the street for help. They just looked at me funny like I'd asked for change, and kept on walking past. My begging turned into one long anguished scream, and my mother was shaking her head, telling me not to make so much fuss, that it wasn't worth it. I started screaming at her, then, telling her that it wasn't fair. Then, before anything else happened, she died, and a lot of blood gushed out of her mouth. That's when I woke up.

I slept in my clothes again. I have to quit doing that. I have a permanent seam in my left leg from my jeans. I'm going to go take a shower.

5:03 p.m.

I took a really nice shower, and then I put on a pot of coffee, and the grey album. I used to not like this record, but now I really do. I don't feel the need to skip ahead to track three. I put the disk on shuffle today, and I'm getting "Blue Blue Ocean", one of Mac's best seascapes. *Silhouettes and a vulture hoping he's gonna pick the bones of you and me . . .* What are you trying to say here, Mac? Skip to the next random track? Okay, I will. "Lost and Found." Ugh, I hate this song. I do right now, anyway. Maybe this isn't such a good album for right now. Maybe silence would be better. Coffee's made.

5:50 p.m.

Best not. It's not for me to enjoy or not enjoy. It is mine to listen and learn and sing. Start at the beginning and recite to keep the future at bay. I want my mother to be okay.

7:38 p.m.

Lise home. She got a load of mail today—more videos, some cards, a letter from her father which she's reading intently now, trying to concentrate through the haze of whiskey on an empty stomach. She's putting on weight. Fortunately it looks kind of good on her, but still, I haven't noticed her getting heavier like this before in all the time we've known each other. Meanwhile I get thinner and thinner, though I've been trying to eat more. I feel terrible, though, because it's Lise's food. I just don't want anything enough to leave the house to get it. I'd much rather sit still and try to think. Lise brought me food tonight, though, leftovers from her dinner out with the Pronto regional manager, leftover Thai chicken curry over rice. Good. I thanked her with the correct measure of cheer and contrition, but she didn't really respond, she went straight for her mail and the bottle and the pipe. I pity her, really. But I'm grateful. I think I'll hug her.

11:12 p.m.

The food was a good idea.

Lise is falling asleep, again in front of the flickering telly. I've turned the sound off and changed it to a channel that still transmits static—if I disconnect the VCR cable, I can keep it from displaying that blank, peaceful blue screen that, for some reason, I find really menacing and uncomfortable. Static is beautiful. Leftover radiation from the dawn of creation, sparkles of starstuff, a million patterns apparent all the time, ever changing, ever interesting.

1 a.m., Pioneer Cemetery

The rain has slowed down enough for me to write a bit. It wasn't raining really hard, but enough for me to worry—this paper is a little less durable, and I'm using a Rollerball ink pen. Ideally I won't shed any tears over this diary. I don't think I will. I'm pretty far from weeping right now. I am in love with all of creation, from that tree to that headstone to that writhing, drowning earthworm. I have more in common with you than you know, brother! I too am drowning in the very medium that keeps me alive, I too have been vomited up from my home and have no choice except to desiccate and become food for ruthless birds. If I could save your life, my wormy pal, I would, but it's too late. I can tell by your texture that it's already too late and your delicate balance of fluids has been hopelessly disrupted. Soon you will die. Myself, as well.

And I can hear the earth drinking in the escaping souls of the worms. Listen to it. Listen to that supernatural sound! The earth, sipping and gulping and swallowing! The gastric rumblings of an entire planet, shivering, exhausted after the feed, after being made love to and ejaculated upon by the sky. Aah, it fills me with elation and joy.

4:33 a.m.

Oh well.

Of course, I shouldn't have left. I wanted a soda. I went to the corner store. I got a soda and paid for it with loose change, which was all I had. The guy at the counter gave me shit for paying with loose change, so I flicked my bottlecap at him, and he launched himself across the counter and started throttling me. Fortunately a hollow-eyed junkie came in needing cigarettes, and the counter guy had to let me go. By then I was sitting on the floor, screeching uncontrollably, and the junkie looked at me and said "Fuck, little dude, what'd you do?"

Lise sleeps. The blanket has moved down to cover her feet, leaving her head uncovered. She's sweating in her sleep. Hair stuck to her forehead. Does she know that my neck is raw and black and blue? Does she know that my eyes are in agony from not being able to weep? Does anyone know how fierce this heart is, this heart that pains me until I wish I could wrench it out, the heart that keeps my eyes wide open and my breathing quick and shallow? I'll never sleep again. I knew that I should have avoided soda. It's bad for you.

12 November, waking up

Man, it feels like I've been asleep for days. I kind of have. After the convenience store episode I just grabbed an extra blanket and huddled up in the closet, waiting until I could sleep. And sleep I did. I don't really remember falling asleep, but I do remember waking up, deciding consciousness wasn't worth it, and going back to sleep. How many times did that happen? I got up and peed at some point, it was daylight, I think. That's weird. It's dark in here.

Great dreams, which was why I was so reluctant to come back. I mean *great* dreams. Dreams of utter beauty and terror and astonishment and wonder. All my fantasies came true, sometimes with grave consequence (for example, I conjured up a great dragon with red and gold scales, *très* Pern, and then she disemboweled me with one swipe of her foreclaw), but with that soft, calm reassurance and remoteness that only exists in dreams. The worst part is, when I wake up, the good parts evaporate and I'm still *here*, I'm still *this*.

Lise home. I hear her cleaning the bathroom. Now the kitchen. She's listening to Haydn, the recording of her mother playing with the Seattle Symphony Orchestra. It's only the second or third time I've ever heard her play it, and it was recorded before we met. Her mother is a really superb cellist, but not such a good mom. She left when Lise was only nine, just old enough to take it personally. If I were Lise, I'd tell people my mother was dead. She did, for a while. She said that to me, only one of the lies that she would continue to feed me over the years.

Lise = Lies. Only the bad parts of us are left. It's my fault.

I want something to eat, but I don't know what's there. I would order a pizza, but I don't want to use the phone—if I pick it up, it might ring, and I'd have to answer it, and it might be my mom or someone from Link-Up or the police, wanting to know where I got those pictures, if I could help them in a sting operation; they'd haul me in and then drug test me and they'd find the $\Delta 9$-tetra-hydra-cannabinol that I excrete in every single pee. And then I'd be sent up the river. Penitentiary. Solitary confinement. Forever.

Nice dark quiet box like this one. Hmmm.

November 14th, night

Oh thank God!

I thought I was going to kill myself, I really did—you went missing for a whole day and night and I searched everywhere, even out in the hall, upstairs hall, the laundry room with its cowl of bloodless cobwebs, the lobby where the government spies drop off their covert messages to Lise in the form of Soloflex videos and little plastic packets of fabric softener (and *they know who I am*!!), I searched through the kitchen, in the pantry, in the cupboards, in the little flap where the linoleum curls up near the sink, in the sink, under the sink, in the lens covering the kitchen light; I looked in the bathroom, in bathtub, vanity, medicine cabinet, under the bathroom rug, into random bottles of shampoo, lotion, and sexual lubricant. Lise came home and freaked, and handed it to me, it having been locked in the old mailbox slot that I had always assumed was broken or nailed shut. "Just take it, for fuck's sake!" she said. "I thought it might help you if you didn't have this staring you in the face twenty-four hours a day! Just do me one favor please—call your mother and talk to her. If you do nothing else, please do that." And a lot more unfair and horrible and untrue things.

I promised her I'd call my mother. I have no intention of calling my mother. My mother has nothing to do with anything—if anything, she's with *them*. She's a homeowner, a business owner, one of the capitalists, one of them. She has to protect her own self-interests at all costs. It's not her fault. But she cannot offer me any help, and if you can't help me, you might as well harm me.

Only I help myself.

Are you alive? Should I talk to you? Talking out loud isn't working for me.

11:15 p.m.

Tell Lise to go away and leave me alone. I'm trying to take a bath.

1:02 a.m.

I wonder if I can get a really cheap black and white TV. That'd be cool to have in my closet—I could just watch static all day, drinking in the radiation, reading the sensitive messages in the hieroglyphs. There they are now—sound off, Bunnymen on (quietly), hands and eyes and smiles and snarls weaving up out of the storm at me, and then retreating. I can read their expressions for that split second, and if a picture is worth a thousand words, and a picture of a being is worth ten thousand words, the people in the static are worth millions upon millions of words—as many words as there are subatomic particles in the galaxy. All the quarks and bosons that are sitting here and feeling searing pain in the temples and back, the ones that are shaped like girl's feet, sticking from underneath a quilt—made of the same substance. The faces of the static leap off the screen and swirl around my mind just long enough to transform, and turn into Lise's beautiful, pink, tired feet. I am experiencing the true vastness of the universe, more fully than any man has ever experienced it.

What am I? I am nothing. A skeleton white boy with hair reminiscent of the fat Elvis, in boxer shorts, thermal underwear, barefoot, all gooseflesh and fingernails chewed to the quick and yellow with nicotine, a face like the Grim Reaper at Miller Time. Poor fuck. But I am all there is. I am a universe at once self-contained, tiny, and infinite.

15 November, 7:13 p.m. (?)

Should I believe the clock? I am awake, and Lise is not here. I woke myself up with a jerk. No dreams. No verbal ones, anyway—nothing I can express with words. I wonder where she is. She's usually home by now no matter what. I should get something to eat while the getting is good.

9:45 p.m.

She's still not here.

I ate some soft, going-bad oranges and a bowl of cereal and some leftover mashed potatoes, and drank a pot of coffee, and took a shower. The heat is on, so I'm able to sit around the apartment in boxer shorts and a T-shirt and socks. There was a message from my mom on the answering machine, which I deleted. I didn't listen to the actual content; just her tone of voice was unpleasant enough that my heart started pounding in my head. It's no good. At least Lise won't know Marion called.

11:00 p.m.

Oh leaping flaming shit. I went to get Lise's mail and she was THERE when I returned with my arms loaded with little packages, barcodes, iridescent hologram fibers, catalogues, and government microfilms. She jumped when she saw me and I dropped her mail all over the floor. She told me to go out to the store and get her a six pack of Mickey's, and she didn't seem to understand what was going on when I laughed. She's outside the bathroom right now and tapping on the door and saying something over and over, I don't know what, I have the water running in the tub and in the sink. I am shaking myself to pieces, wouldn't that be perfect. Shake and wake and bake. Shake shake shake shake shake. Shakey shakey shakey laughy Mikey shakeyboyshake shakedogshake

~~GOAWAYGOAWAYGOAWAYGOAWAYGOAWAYGOAWAY~~
~~GOAWAY~~

There are ten, no, eleven pages that are scratched out here; a meticulous hand scrawled perfect exact circles and crosshatches through all of the text. It is completely obscured; only the above letters remain, the rest choked out of existence with a few hours of diligent work. The writing continues on the next intact page, with the same pen used to redact the previous pages, in a careful, precise hand that bears only the slightest resemblance to what came on the last legible page. Why didn't I just tear the pages out?

2 December, 2:15 p.m.

Lise and I are at the Convention Center Denny's.

This morning we woke up at the same time, in the same bed, touching each other. We woke up and kissed. She gazed at me and said "Are you okay?" and I was able to tell her honestly, "Yeah."

When Lise was in the shower, I called Mom and we talked. The bookstore is doing pretty well—she's thinking about hiring yet another person and only working twenty hours a week, taking the extra time to take classes. She didn't bug me about "where I've been."

That's good, because I wouldn't know what to tell her. I don't know what happened, exactly. I think I was just incredibly stressed because of the whole work thing. Whatever. I don't care. I'm here now. It's as if I was covered with mud, and now I'm washed. I understand the religious imagery of washing and cleansing and baptism now; my fish-belly white skin seems perfectly right.

It's amazing how long my hair is. I've never had hair this long before. I can really truly make a ponytail now—a real ponytail, not a yuppie-scum microtail. I'm rocking a ponytail now, a rubber band and a shoelace as a ribbon. I look like a young, dazed priest. I *am* kind of cute. Redred lips and whitewhite skin and big, bloodshot eyes the color of the "burnt umber" crayon, my absolute least favorite color in the box. But today, it's okay; I can look at it and I think of all the crayons, the gradient beauty of a newly opened sixty-four.

Lise is in the bathroom. Poor Lise. She's been so patient. She works six days a week now, and most of the time she goes into work at ten in the morning and gets off work at ten at night. She has more money than she knows what to do with, but she barely has time to breathe. She's going to take me shopping today to make it up to me for neglecting me. I wish I could give her something to make it up to her for not even being alive, human, conscious, for the last God knows how long (there's only so far back in the journal I went before my hand got tired this morning; I did it while I was on the phone with my mother). Whatever. It's in the past now. And now my beautiful lover returns from the ladies' restroom, gorgeous in fuzzy black cashmere cardigan and skirt too short for the blustery cold weather, smiling. Beautiful Lise, smiling.

[different handwriting, same pen.]

I love you Squire and I'm so glad you're back.

6:30pm

Lise bought me *Crocodiles* and *Ocean Rain* used on CD, and also a nice red ski sweater that makes me look like a superbly flat-chested girl. I hugged her and kissed her and danced around, in public, in the Square, where she gave me the gifts. Technically they're birthday presents; she'd planned them before my birthday, but didn't have time to get them (besides, she admits, she was pretty mad at me). I actually embarrassed her. This is definitely a first.

I was stunned by the complete lack of reaction to me. I felt like I'd just had radical plastic surgery, but nobody seemed to notice me. The waitress at Denny's refilled my coffee cup about six times without realizing how downright weird that was. And nobody on the street looked at me particularly, even with the red sweater on—I mean, that thing stands out like a spotlight. Like blood in snow. Lise says it looks striking.

I'm cooking for her right now, while she rolls a fat blunt and watches television. I actually think I'll smoke pot tonight. I've already drunk alcohol. We had the last inch of vodka left in the bottle from summertime—I can't believe it's lasted so long. It stung my mouth and it wasn't particularly special or nice, but I didn't mention it. I'm waiting for pasta to boil and then I'm going to toss it with this cool pesto Lise found which has artichoke and cilantro in it—it sounds good. And a salad, and some hot rolls, which I think I've forgotten and they're burning

1:12 a.m.

"Stop writing," she says. But I want to say something, to put it down permanently, in case I'm liable to forget how wonderful everything is. She's smiling at me from the bed, eyes foggy with dope and endorphins. Neurotransmitter Boy has been here and completely debilitated my girlfriend with his evil, delightful ways. Perhaps there's a feminine equivalent of blue balls—it seemed as though she was saving up all her orgasms for the next time she got to let them out, and humble me in comparison. I haven't even been jacking off recently, strangely enough—sexuality, even in a sick and twisted and loveless form, has been a stranger to me. I've really only been inside my own cerebral cortex, and even the hindbrain takes a backseat to that (no pun intended).

Aah, it's not a bad life, all told. Full of complex carbohydrates (only some of them burnt), stoned (very stoned!), a space shuttle mission on the television, and the Bunnymen (pleasure of pleasures!) on the stereo, repeating softly. Amazing how good it sounds even at near sub-sonic levels.

The blue curvature of the earth softly lights Lise's face as she closes her eyes and rolls over onto her side, away from me. Her chewed-off fingernails are tiny dark-red baroques. I can smell her vaginal juices all over my fingers, even though I washed my hands afterward. She begged me to finger-fuck her until my whole arm went numb, but I gave and gave, and she came until the tears streamed over her cheeks. How could I stop?

So now she's asleep and I can be free. I hate having to hide this from Lise, but she really doesn't trust the journal, even though I've assured her that I have it under control. I can't believe she went so far as to hide it from me. How ridiculous! I thought I was going to tear the place apart with my bare hands. I had stuff from the entire apartment in the middle of the living room, I had living room stuff in the bathroom. It was pretty obvious what I'd been doing. I remember that night with great clarity—I was crying and shaking and there was drool on my chin and my hair stung my eyes and I was going through the telephone book page by page, muttering to myself "I have to find it, I have to find it," and I'd taken off all my clothes just in case I had hidden it somewhere upon my person. Yeah, it must have looked pretty bad. But goddamn it, it seemed logical at the time. Why should I trust the stupid links of logic? They've let me down before. I have learned not to trust anything. Anything. All of it is deceptive—truly Buddhist, I'm becoming. But I'm serious. Buddhists understand that all of this is a dream. All of it except my ideas, my ability to lay them out in print form. Printing. Look at my handwriting, isn't it lovely? I've been working on it, mentally, I think, for the last couple of nights where I just crashed and slept and woke up just long enough to stare at the walls and the sounds coming out of the walls, the disconnected souls in between the molecules of air. My handwriting is perfect and beautiful and the lettering itself is artwork. I am a calligrapher of souls.

At the witching hour between this glorious day and the next, I can feel myself coming alive.

5 December, 10:03 p.m.

From point A to Point B is not always what it seems. Sometimes it spirals and sometimes it goes dash-dash-dash straight across and sometimes it skips around—always in groups of five, like a leopard's spots, that's what old Seagal taught me in those long slow golden afternoons where my back was screaming and my hands felt like blood would run from underneath the fingernails! A leopard's spots! Old Seagal! How did he know?

Sensei Seagal, who would hit me if my crosshatching wasn't good enough.

Notions, notions, notions, all of it is notions, none of this need bother me, all those ants on the street, sleek and sliding forms like red and blue and white wet dolphins, coasting through hydroplane rain—all of it is imaginary and in my mind.

Dark apartment, bathroom rug, rain, glass lens on the floor, broken eyeglasses. The page is a smear. I like it. My lettering is still precise like machine printing. I am a machine.

Back to the drawing floor.

10 December, morning

No idea what time it is. I'm in the closet. My ski sweater makes a cozy pillow and I have a nice blanket and it's warm and sweet and my breath makes the air bearable.

I can't believe I slipped. That day. Denny's, for God's sake. The waitress poisoned my coffee and molested Lise in the bathroom—she had bruises on her arms. That *night*. It all seemed so fantastic, so right, so fated to be. How stupid could I have been? I didn't think I could get any stupider, but apparently, anything is possible when it comes in groups of five, like leopard spots. Five or six. NO, FIVE. And I spoke to my mother. How stupid! She called the postal service and made them send me something and the mailman gave me this smile and asked me "How it was going". Fuck you, man! You know how it's going. You know everything about me. I had no choice but to take the envelope away because he was watching me, and I brought it upstairs and put it in the middle of the kitchen table and came in here. I hope I haven't gotten poisoned or dosed by handling the stupid thing. It's white and plain and perfect for hiding things. It's probably for Lise anyway, it's just got my name on it so that the postal service could confirm who I am. *Jesus!!* How could I have been so stupid? And I was stupid in the Square across from the Courthouse, of all places. What I need is a time machine so I can go back and erase that whole thing. Well, at least I won't make the same mistake again. I like it in here.

10:12 says the microwave

It's morning. I have to get up and go now. I'm taking a minute to log in, between putting on the shoes and tying the shoes, just so that I know I'm here and I can get a good gauge on the time. I was lying curled up in the closet for a long time, thinking about sleeping, and then thinking about other things, and then I noticed that it was light and Lise was gone and I'd been staring at the ceiling all night with my head all abuzz. Enough. Gotta get going with my day. I haven't a moment to lose.

10:32am says the digital clock outside the bank

Making good time. I should stop somewhere on the way and get some coffee and cigarettes. There's something on my arms and I can't figure out what it is. I think it's on the page too. I think it's something to do with the bus.

10:34 on the bank

Waiting for the next bus. Obviously the bus driver didn't understand that I'm in a fuckin' hurry—what does he think I have all these CDs for, do I look like a DJ? I was just trying to get that pink stuff off my sleeve and off my stuff. The driver yelled at me as he slammed the door in my face "It's the light! It's just the light, you crazy kid!" Like he would even know. He wasn't even there. I hate it when people assume they know why something is happening when they don't know.

Fuck this, this is too long to wait. I'm going to walk.

11:15 says the clock on the wall of the shop

Stopped for a drink of water. Sun out. Tingles on the itchy back of my neck. I can still kind of feel the pink slime on my skin even though it barely touched my skin. It was like I was immersed in it up to the neck. I'm glad I walked. It was good to see the river. It's a solution, if need be.

2:32 says the clock on the bank

What a score!

The guy at the store gave me a lot for that crappy music—enough to buy three copies of *Ocean Rain* on vinyl, one on tape: two copies of *Crocodiles* on CD, the "Lips like Sugar" 12", *The Peel Sessions*, two tape copies of *Songs to Learn And Sing* (Lise's favorite Bunnymen album, so she can have one and I'll keep the other), and all the copies of the grey album they had—I think it's something like three copies on CD and two on tape and one, badly scratched, on vinyl. The salesgirl looked at me kind of funny when I was in line, but I wasn't sure if it was because of the Bunnymen, or because of the fact that being tired from walking and being so out of shape I was panting and wheezing the whole time I was in the store.

I have something like fifty dollars left, even after getting just the bare essentials. I should buy cigarettes, and coffee. This is way better than having a job.

I don't know what time it is.

I lost my bus pass somewhere—that bus driver dickweed probably stole it while I was incapacitated, now I have to replace that too. I should drop by the bank.

3:15, says the driver.

I feel a lot better now; I'm on a bus being driven by a nice-looking, calm, silent black lady with thick braids and thick plastic-framed glasses. There's nobody else on the bus with me; I'm going the opposite direction from everyone. I'm going towards the right place, and I don't know where everyone else is going. I feel better than I have in ages. Maybe I should clean up the apartment. Lise would probably appreciate that. Maybe I can do the ironing and the hand washables and water the plant and take down the recycling and cook dinner and won't she be surprised! I dunno. I can't figure her out lately. Hopefully the presents will cheer her up.

7:07 p.m.

Oh well fuck shit blimey.

Lise read me the riot act. I like that phrase—so much more descriptive than "yelling at me." Reading the riot act sounds so much cooler. She was a one-woman riot, complete with looting. She let me have it about selling "her" CDs, all "her" precious CDs full of crap that we never listened to anyway. She didn't care about the tape I bought her, since she's already got a copy. Of course, this is an actual studio original and not just a crappy dubbed tape from high school, but she doesn't care. She's upset about the stupid Doors vinyl and the stupid Cocteau Twins box set and the rare this and the rare that. And then she had the gall to ask me where the rest of the money went, and I showed her the coffee and the TVs and the bus passes. I bought one and a spare for myself and a spare for her, and I bought ten pounds of black French roast and two television sets from Fairly Honest Bill's. They don't show TV, which is good, but they do show static, which is good.

Now I'm all confused. We actually do need all that stuff. *We* do. If she loses her bus pass, won't she be happy to know she's got another one right there? And, I mean, shit, I just sold all the other music *I* own, but if I lost the only copy I had of *Crocodiles*, I'd go out of my mind. If I don't hear "Rescue" at least once a day my head will just explode; that's all there is to it. It's good to have a backup of the important things, triple redundancies, first thing I learned when learning to use a computer. Stuff dies. Make a backup. At least one; preferably several redundant ones. I mean, shit; I had to buy that stuff. And she doesn't get it. It was my money too.

She took my Walkman and threw it out the window onto the courtyard stones and I could hear it break. Good thing I don't care. It's not that important to me anymore. I'm happy to listen to music at home.

And doesn't she love TV? What the fuck.

11 December, post-midnight

Lise and I didn't even fight. She just came in and went straight to bed without speaking to me. Yesterday we fought. Yesterday we fought terribly. She told me I was being hysterical and unreasonable and she'd hoped I was on my way out. I told her she was an idiot for ever believing that I'd be all stupid and normal again, and wasn't this better? Wasn't it better to be honest? She was mad about me sleeping on my sweater rather than wearing it, and for taking the best blanket. I told her to find the shittiest blanket ever and give that to me, so she let me keep my original choice. She even shook me by the shoulders, but that made my head pound so much that I yelled and she let me go. That was after she threw my Walkman out the window. I thought she was going to throw the new TVs out the window, too, so I stood in front of them and growled. Her arms tensed up and I knew, just knew that she was going to hit me. But she didn't. I don't know why not; I'd have beaten my ass. Beat it to death and thrown it out the window.

Tonight there was none of that. She came in and went to bed. She took off her clothes, but not her underwear, got under the quilt, and turned out the lamp. She sighed three or four times, turned over once, and slept. I watched her from the relative safety of the bathroom mirror. I'm sitting on the cold bare linoleum, staring at the curly piece under the sink that stretches up grotesquely like a dragon's tooth, like the claw from my dream that gently caressed my belly and caused my innards to slide out like so many Thanksgiving gizzards.

I actually went outside again today. I went to the convenience store for cigarettes. I go through a lot. Lise buys cartons of Winstons, but I sometimes smoke a lot and run through the carton before she gets home. She left me, on the table, a twenty-dollar bill and a note that said "Get cigarettes. This is your money. I cashed your check from the end of November—the rest of it is mine." I don't understand—what check? What money? I don't remember getting anything. But I bought the cigarettes and a packet of potato chips. The Asian woman who works there looked at me really strangely today, too. I am glad I didn't wear the sweater, even though it was cold and tiny cubes of ice were falling down on my head. I went out in my regular clothes—black T-shirt, black jeans, canvas tennis shoes. My hair is really long. I bet she can tell that I have these thoughts. Maybe I should stop going there.

15 December, night time

In the bath.

Thrilling, this feeling, of not being contained within myself, of having no boundaries. I melt in the water. I'm going to watch some TV later. See what's on Birth of the Universe TV.

16 December, still night, same night

The people in the static are speaking to me. When I got out of the bath Lise was asleep and so I made a pot of coffee and turned the static on. I watched for a couple of hours without effect or message, then I could hear the voices, softly muttering, the patterns and images coalescing at the same time. I wanted another pot of coffee, but I haven't been able to move in case I miss something terribly important. Things I've made out so far:

"Keep it down" (many times). "Sleep" (interspersed with a kind of gentle whispering—that word repeated sharply and distinctly many times over). "Glass." And above all, "Wait."

Three watching unblinking glaucous eyes. My hands are cold and slick with anticipation.

My heart is pounding.

I am sick, but I am vigilant.

11:45 a.m.

This is for all the high school counsellors;

this is for all the OLCC Nazis who card me with delight in bars;

this is for all the Robs and Melissas;

this is for the kids who didn't get to go to Yale because their parents made too much money;

this is for the indolent superstars of art;

this is for all those people who laughed at me when I found out the Bunnymen had broken up;

this is for crumbs in bed;

this is my exhortation of rage, contained, I mustn't speak out or I will be instantly crushed by cosmic justice; that cosmic justice the said I should be born so that I could tear out chunks of my own hair and arrange them on the kitchen table,

born so that I could suffer and err—

those sulfuric mailmen,

those catalytic checkers-out,

those concrete-layers,

those grinders of wheat, spinners of nylon, devourers of Sizzlean,

those bright-eyed, those passengers, those miserable freaks who are almost—so very close—to knowing what I feel, except that they can't, because they're not me.

I'm alone in this.

Juba could be dead. Mom could be dead. I don't know. I can't know. I could be deceived.

"Wait," it says.

17 December, 5:15 a.m.

Pouring a bowl of cereal is so incredibly stressful. You're making this temporal contract with yourself—when you pour the milk on, you know you have only a very limited amount of time to eat all the cereal before it goes soggy. Will you pass this test, or fail it? So you stand there in the kitchen, milk box poised in space, drawing a detailed pocketwatch in your mind, you press the button—and pour. Or don't pour. I couldn't do it just now—I just got so worried that I'd fail and that my cereal would go soggy instantaneously. I don't trust the milk anymore—it's making the same cereal soggy faster and faster all the time. Last time I got a bowl it was soggy by the time I got to the kitchen table. Milk—who needs milk, anyway? I'm probably lactose intolerant anyway and I've been slowly killing myself all this time without knowing it. And cereal is for little fucking kids. I should have toast or something manly like bacon and eggs. Fuck this cereal shit. It's toast from here on out. I guess that means I have to buy bread, though. Fuck. Maybe I can get Lise to go get bread. I think I've got the money, and if I tell her she can keep the change, maybe she'll go get it for me. Okay. All right.

6:42 a.m.

DAMN IT. I forgot all about the fact that the makers of potato chips are also thwarting my every move—I got hungry waiting for Lise to wake up, and I found a bag of some kind of orange-flavored chips and I tried to open them and eat its contents. But Mr. Lay, whoever he is, cleverly designed these packets so that I, Michael Squire, cannot open them neatly, silently, as befits a petty thief of other people's lunch bag items. I simply cannot. I've been trying for half an hour. And no, I will not bend to the will of mechanical aids like scissors, or risk a chipped tooth trying to rip the bag open orally. It's a good thing I don't try it, I'd get a face full of orange flavored tear gas all over my face and hands and thermals like the lunchroom scene, that fabulous lunchroom scene that ended me in the nurse's office having a bronchial emergency while an entire elementary school laughed their superior heads off at the weird kid who talks all funny who couldn't even open a bag of chips for Chrissake. Who called them *crisps*. Still laughing. I can hear their laughter ricocheting through the linoleum and the glass and the walls and the body in the bed turning restlessly, as though caught in the same nightmare that I inhabit.

I don't want to cry anymore.

Never mind cereal or chips. The voices are happening again—different voices, drowning out the continuous kiddy laughter. Along with this is a gentle rushing sound full of words I can't make out. And I don't even have the Eyes open. They're asleep. They are coming from somewhere else.

I hate milk and chips and everything of the kind. It made me fall asleep. At the kitchen table, even. I won't sleep anymore, I've decided. Too much can happen when I'm asleep. I might get that final ultimate message from Mac about the end coming (it's almost the 23rd!) and if I were asleep, I'd go up with the rest of these goons. I have to be vigilant and alert and on my toes at all times. Never mind the green circles or the exploding pain in my nasal sinus passages—I must listen, listen, listen.

9:15 p.m. says my digital watch.

I don't hear you, lalalalalala.

I am not listening.

You can't see me, so I don't exist. Go away. Go back to work, since you love it so much. Go back to your bond and toner and Pronto yellow and leave me alone. I'm fine in here. Let me be. I was almost perfect—I was almost at the point at which all things were going to be revealed to me, I was listening between the beats and between the words, and then YOU come home, you shatter everything precious, you're worried about your stupid boom box which isn't that good anyway but does me a lot of good. Don't you worry your pretty little head, Miss Ballard. You'll do fine with just your TV pumping you full of lies and when the time comes you can go with everyone else and I'll walk away from the wreckage. You missed your chance. Go. Away. Go Away Now.

Your stupid clothes are outside. I didn't hurt them. They're right in front of you. Just open your fucking eyes.

Louder, Mac, Will, Les, Pete. Louder.

Yes. ("Won't you come on down to my rescue?" Won't you please, won't you please.)

Yes.

Yes.

No?

No.

Don't end. Don't leave me *alone.*

18 December and I don't care what time it is.

De Freitas is not dead. This is endless and eternal as long as I am here to hear it, as long as I contain soul to be moved by it. There is no Echo.

19 December, is it?

Water? Christ, no! what have I been doing to myself? Water! Water! I haven't been boiling or distilling my water, so God knows what I've been feeding myself—sleep drugs, fluoride, truth potions, drugs to make me humiliate myself in public. No more coffee, then. Shit. No more coffee and no more showers. The only two things that were lifelines between myself and it. No more. No more.

I'm kidding. But seriously. The water tastes awful and I haven't been filtering it and I have no fucking idea what's in it, but I haven't been sleeping lately.

It's five in the morning; I looked at the microwave. Or that's what it said. I don't think I believe it. Whatever! It's dark but for the piss yellow glow of the Leatherworks sign. Whatever time. Winter is darker gray and lighter gray. A sleeping body on the futon, as if it grew there like a fungus. I get up and the fungus is gone, but when I go to drain the snake, it's there again. It is confusing.

Hopefully I'll piss less when I stop drinking water and coffee and milk. Ideally I won't excrete anything at all. There isn't time for it. I have only four more days to get the message and I can't miss a single second. I've listened to "Rescue" 24 hours a day for the last two days and I've missed a couple of moments because I fell asleep. It won't happen again. I got the coffee beans. They're in here with me now. My friends.

Man, are they all gonna be surprised when they see what happens. I almost can't wait except that it means the end of everything, and I already miss my mom and Lise so much that it makes breathing difficult.

December sometime

I don't know the day or the time. If I were still clinging to nonsense I'd say it's the twentieth, but how am I ever to tell? It could be the next millennium or the next eon outside, for all I know, but why should I care? I have everything I need in here. My planet sweet on a silver salver, my walls coated with silver, beautiful . . . and even better, it keeps the faces from coming out of the plaster and talking to me. I can't listen to the voice of the static or the plaster or the between-molecules-of-air because they are telling me lies. They are telling me to sleep and I must not ever listen to them even a little bit because I'm listening to the true message 24 hours a day until the right message comes to me. The metal-reinforced walls will protect me from orbital satellites or static people or the mailman or Marion or the long dresses or the leopard's spots and cowl me in silver and here I will transcend. I will pass beyond this.

Crisps. Fuck this place.

I puked up the coffee beans. There were a lot of them. Now the closet is half its former size. It was the last of the evil in me. Clean now. The last of it is now out of me and now I can focus on my spiritual quest.

If I said I'd lost my way, would you—could you sympathize?

Nothing else. Nothing else. Listen. Listen. *Listen.* Art and feeling and beauty in the lettering. Immortality. We will survive this apocalypse together.

I have the watch. It is 3:18 p.m. The apartment outside is so bright it sickens me. I wish I'd never heard of it. It hurts and my stomach is roiling. But I can hang on. I'm still here.

4:00 p.m.
Still here.

4:30 p.m.
Still here. Still awake. I have to piss, but that's too bad.

5:00 p.m.
I'm OK.

5:30 p.m.
I had to leave the closet to urinate and shit. Now I'm shaking, no matter how loud I have the track turned up, no matter how I wrap myself in the blanket. But I'm still here, by God. The mailmen have come and gone without hurting me. Only a little while longer to go. Please, don't let the phone ring. Please, have mercy.

6:03 p.m.

I must hang on.

6:39 p.m.

Still here. Feeling better. The pile of black vomit is merely interesting to me now.

7:00 p.m.

Got it on the tick. Still here. Apocalypse hasn't started yet, but I'm ready. Voices coming from outside. Ignore them

7:30 p.m.

On the tick again. On the second. I'm ready. The voice hurts. But I'm okay.

8:00:00:00:00 p.m.

Still here.

11:18 p.m.!!! CRAP

Shit, shitfire, fuck, I slipped, and I listened to the voices and let the last traces of water in my body tell me to sleep. And I was too weak. I woke up when the front door opened and I heard Lise cursing. I turned on the Song again and listened to it three or four times and now I feel like I can perhaps breathe again. The headache is terrible. I almost wish it would just end, be over, let me die and let them have me. Why am I hanging on?

11:30:00 p.m.

Still here. Still awake. Never again.

"What happened to my aluminum foil?" Oh, for Mac's sake, shut up.

12:00:00:00:00:00

All is silent. I've let the Song lapse. I want to see if the voices have ceased. Seems they have, for now. I wonder if it's safe to sleep.

No, no, no, whatever I can do to hang in there, whatever I can do, it's good enough, it's worth it, it's worth it, I can do it, I can do it. It's only a little while longer. Let me find the play button—my booklight is very faint now, the batteries running down. It really can't be helped.

12:30:00 a.m.

Still here.

1:00 a.m.

Thirteen o'clock. The witching hour. One of many. I stretch my eyes open with my fingers. But I'm still here and it hasn't started yet. Or at least it's not here yet. It might be just down the street. I am listening for it; the sound of sidewalks and streets and buildings ripped and crushed into nothingness, a vicious smiting from a vengeful . . . I don't know. That's the scariest part; I don't even know what's behind this. I just know it's coming. Today's the day.

1:15

Oh fuck Christ oh God help!

1:30

I'm still here. I hear the voices, but I'm shutting them out.

2:00:00 a.m.

Second wind! I've taken to scribbling warning evocations into the aluminum foil walls themselves—I am surrounded by protective incantations. Why didn't I think of this before? Words from heaven, from beyond, the sacred text, the sacred song. Holy, holy, holy, better than anything ever created before. I have

148

worked my way around the wainscotting and am now working my way up. This is so awesome. But back to work!

2:30 a.m.

I am about an inch up the walls now. My heartbeat is the same beat as the song, my headache thrumming twice as fast. There's blood under the fingernails of my right hand (why hadn't I been left-handed! Then I would have been known as sinister from a young age and they would have left me out to the wolves, the leopards, the elements!) and my hair stings when it flops into my eyes. There's sick on the knees of my jeans and it's cold and sticky and it smells—well, it smelled like vomited coffee beans. I wonder if I could sell this on the gourmet coffee black market? If they sell coffee bean animal shit, surely they can sell coffee-bean vomit?

3: 00 am

Can't write no more. My hand is killing me. Apologies Sensei. I will sit still and listen and wait for the message, or the destruction, to come. Either one would be welcome. I just want this to be over. I'm so sorry for everything I've done. I don't want to hurt anybody else; just take me. Please.

3:15 a.m.

help

3:30 a.m.

help

3:45 a.m.

help

4:00 a.m.

HELP!! Goddamn it, why aren't you listening? Do I need to sing the Beatles? Do I need to speak aloud? Help me, help me, help help help.

Before it's too late.

It is too late.

I'm screaming and no one hears it. They don't get it. Help help help. Help. Fuck. I have to get this out of my head.

I have to get this out of my head

I have to get this out of my head

I have to get this OUT of my HEAD

I have to get them out of my head

I have to get it out

I have to get it out

I have to get it out

I have to get it out

I have to

have to

have to

rescue

5:00:00 a.m. on the tick

No, I'm all right. I'm fine now. I'm back to writing in the silver. Bailed on my worst fear. No no no no no wrong song. FUCK. I screwed it up. Now I have to start over from the beginning.

5:30

My head. Oh, God. No water in me to come out of my eyes. Maybe I'm close. I hope I drop dead soon.

Six!

I smell bleach! And ozone! I particularly smell ozone. It's a good smell. A real smell. A machine smell It's covering up the coffee smell of vomit. I have a groove in my forehead worn from pressing my face into the stereo speakers. I am covered with a film of Echo and the Bunnymen that will never be washed away, no matter how much poisoned water they sluice over me.

I hear the streets crumbling. It's here. IT'S HERE.

Nine something in the morning—I don't have time to look— but there they are, I can hear them outside. I can hear them doing something to the doorknob, trying to get through the paper I've jammed into the lock. Heh! I hear voices, I hear a name, I hear—

NO! They took it! There's no more music! You won't get me, goddamn it, you won't get ME—

Even dead my soul will live on in these pages and in the soul of this song—

you can't get me m___

otherfucker you cant get

The last couple of pages in the notebook are reduced to shreds shrinking into the binding, as if trying to hide. There are tiny brown spots on the inside back cover that are almost definitely specks of blood. I don't remember their source.

AFTER

A big, dark, immobile gap that I don't remember. I might not ever.

I do remember someone cutting my fingernails. Someone moved my face from side to side and touched me with little spines that stung. My neck felt like all the bones had been removed. I wanted to go back to sleep, and I said so.

After a gray, dizzy, not-sleep space, I opened my eyes to an unfamiliar room, about forty feet by twenty, with six beds in it, three on each side. Each bed contained a man. I walked past each bed, silently, and looked at the men in the beds. Some of them had grey hair and some had no hair and some had blond or brown hair and beards. The two men on the side where I was had their eyes closed, one with black skin and one with white skin and two dark marks on either side of his nose. He was snoring. His lips were dry and scaly and he had a tooth missing in the front. On the other side, there was one man with his face jammed into the pillow, one man on his back, eyes open, staring up at the ceiling, and one man on his side, wearing glasses, his eyes also open, looking at the squares of blue milky light, crisscrossed with thick wires.

I stopped in my tracks and looked at the guy in glasses. He looked at me. "What are you doing up, kid?" he asked me, his voice a whisper.

I asked him if I was dreaming, but he didn't seem to hear me. I went over to the first man with his eyes open, and I watched a hand appear and poke him in the shoulder—a long, white hand, glowing in the milky blue light. He was not staring at the ceiling, but at the square of light, where the other man was looking.

The man in glasses laughed and spoke again. "You get up because of the moonlight?" he said. "It's sure keeping Harris awake. Look at 'im. God knows what's going on inside his head, huh? I know I can't sleep when there's a full moon outside. I can *hear* it. I can hear it in my sleep, I don't care how many pills they give me, I can always hear it." He began to shout. "*I can hear it!*"

The man staring at the window didn't so much as flinch.

The black man began to groan. "Shuddup, Lewis," he groaned.

The man in glasses raised his arms, rose out of the bed, and went to the square of light, looked out, and kept on shouting, a long wordless howl that ended in laughing.

"Go to fuckin' sleep, Lewis," said the black man.

The snoring man didn't stir.

"You're gonna get all of us in trouble, Lewis."

Yellow light burst and spilled into the room. A man came through the yellow light—a very big man in a yellow shirt and green sweatpants. "You cats go to sleep now, hear?" he said. He came in and poked the man in glasses back towards his bed; the man in glasses stopped his laughing and yelling and quietly got back into bed and pulled the blanket over him. He did not, however, take off his glasses. The black man thanked the big man in the sweatpants and covered himself up.

Not sweatpants; scrubs.

"What's up with you, little dude? Go back to bed. Don't let Lewis bother you. You having trouble sleeping?" The big man came over to me and put his thick, warm hand on my shoulder. He turned me around until all I could see was the bed. I sat on it, then drew my knees up to my chest. My heartbeat roared in my ears. The big man fished in a pocket of his scrubs, drew out a bottle, tapped a small blue pill into his palm, and handed it to me. Automatically, like I'd been trained since birth, I took the pill, and a cup of water, and swallowed. "That's the ticket. Now, try to get back to sleep. You don't have to sleep if you don't want to, but you'll feel a lot better if you sleep."

I looked at the edge of my blanket, watching the yellow light shrink and die away, leaving only the cold blue light. The man with glasses laughed softly to himself, then started snoring. A circle edged into the square of light—white, glowing, like tooth. I lay back on my bed and looked at the white circle, noting the grey stains on its surface, watching it smear slowly across the sky.

After another blank, I was brought to see Shandy.

The corners of her mouth were drawn up and pinched together, making little pockets, pouches of smooth skin, slightly rough around the different skin of the lips. There was a little pimple inside my mouth that I bit into until I tasted just a trace of blood. I was dressed in soft, faded plaid flannel. Pajamas from a thrift store, I could tell.

"Good morning, Michael."

Her hands were folded together in her lap on a smooth plane of black fabric. She had a paler strip of skin on one of her fingers right as they folded into the palm part of the hand itself. Her hands were very smooth and pale, almost as pale as mine, and she had no paint on her fingernails.

"My name is Shandy O'Grady. Is that funny? I notice you smiled."

I shook my head.

"It is a funny name. I kind of like it. Please call me Shandy. I like your name too, actually—Michael Squire. Do you go by Mike, or Michael?"

My feet were bare and bony, and the spaces between my toes were scrupulously clean. Even my toenails were clean, but kind of longer than I liked them. I began to worry at the keratin, tearing it off easily. Obviously I hadn't been getting enough calcium.

"Do you know where you are?"

I ran my fingers through my hair, and looked at her desk. It was cheap school-issue, with some magazines on it, stacks of paper, a can of Coca-Cola, a stapler, a box of paper clips. The carpet was puce and grey and very short, with a kind of arrowhead pattern on it. This was not a nice place. Everything looked desperate and cheap.

154

My hair felt rough and coarse. It didn't want to stay off my face. I took off my glasses and wiped my face. My glasses were crudely repaired with black electrical tape on both earpieces.

"Do you know what day it is?"

I didn't have any extra toenail left, and my fingernails were too short to chew. Instead I bit off the thick dead skin around the edges of my fingernails.

"Michael, why don't you say something?"

"'Cos I'm sick of talking," I said impatiently. My throat hurt and I coughed.

She blinked at me. "How can you be sick of talking? You haven't spoken ten words in a week."

My head spun with questions. A week? Have I been here a week? What is this? Who are you? Why does Lewis bawl and scream? Who is *he*? I couldn't speak; my throat hurt too much, my tongue too thick, a heavy sense of shame settling over me like a lead vest.

Her hair caught the light from the window outside. Outside it was all white and grey and blue, but lit up, luminous, almost magical. Her hair was flaming, intense red and put up sloppily with some rubber bands, chopsticks, combs. Her eyes were greyish green and she was wearing makeup over freckles, which is why her mouth looked dry around her lips. On the floor there was a small divot in the carpet, where her desk had been moved to the right, and somehow, I said, "Nobody fucking listens, anyway."

"Well, I'm listening." She paused, waiting for me to speak again. I said nothing. "Do you know where you are?" she asked again, her voice showing no sign of impatience.

"I'm obviously in a hospital," I said.

"Do you know what hospital?"

"No."

"You're at Providence in the inpatient psych wing. You're a psychiatric inpatient. You've been here for a week. Do you remember that?"

"No. I don't remember any of it."

"That's pretty serious, Michael. You're not doing so well. We are trying some medications that should help you start feeling better, but you've got to talk to me, and tell me what's going on."

"Oh," I said. "I don't know what's going on," I added.

She took a deep breath. "Do you remember how you got here?"

My toes were still clean and my feet were getting cold. My entire body began to shake. "I want to go lie down," I said.

"In a little while. You're all right."

"I'm falling asleep," I said honestly. "I can't focus my eyes."

"Try, Michael. You can go lie down later. Right now, let me know. What's on your mind?"

"I don't know what happened," I said. My eyes hurt. "You took my music away."

"I didn't do that, Michael," said Shandy. "I wasn't there."

"But you're one of them," I said.

She shook her head. "Who are they?" she said.

"I gotta go to sleep," I said, shaking mine right back. "I'm really sorry. I really haven't been sleeping."

"You've been sleeping most of the time for the last few days," she explained. But her voice was gentle. "We can cut today's visit short, but I will see you tomorrow. Do you want me to bring you anything?"

"Uh . . . some cigarettes."

"Okay, I'll bring cigarettes. Any particular brand?"

"I don't care," I said, and I didn't.

I went out into the hall, and a stocky black man in pink scrubs took my arm gently with his thick, blunt hand. His fingernails were glossy and well-trimmed. He led me by the arm around a couple of corners and into a dark hall faintly colored by the sound of electric lights in the ceiling. The man gave me a paper cup of colored pills and a paper cup of water. "Hope ya feel better tomorrow," he said, his voice so kind that it made me start crying.

"You look better today. I brought you your cigarettes," Shandy said the next day, "but you can't smoke in here. I think we should go outside and smoke. Put these on, it's pretty cold out there."

She handed me a jacket, a scarf, and a hat—all of them familiar. The jacket was mine, and the scarf and hat were Lise's. We went into a courtyard with benches set up, trees in the middle, cylinders of cement to put your butts in. It was wet and grey and cold and the short grass in the courtyard glistened with condensation. Shandy lit me a cigarette and watched me as I stood, smoking desperately. "Do you mind if I smoke?" she asked me.

"No," I said, shivering already, but feeling good. "You go right ahead."

"How do you feel today?" she asked.

"Awake," I said.

"You look," she continued, raising her eyebrows, "so much more *present* than you did yesterday. You were barely there yesterday. And the day before that you didn't even notice that I was in the room."

"And before that?" I asked.

"Before that, you were pretty drugged up. It takes your body a while to get used to these meds sometimes. You were given haloperidol initially. It's a very potent narcoleptic, and you just conked out for days. I've seen it happen before, otherwise I'd have been worried." She lit a cigarette of her own and exhaled slowly and luxuriously.

"So I'm on antipsychotics?"

"Amongst other things."

"Am I psychotic?" I asked quietly.

She smiled gently. "I don't think so," she replied. "We're medicating right now to see how you respond so that we can get closer to a diagnosis. I think you definitely *were* psychotic. For a little while there." She gave a factual little nod. "Brief psychotic episodes are not incredibly uncommon, and they may or may not be indicative of a different underlying disorder. I'm not sure yet, though. It's good to see you up and alert today, though. I decreased the dosage of Zyprexa to see if that'd wake you up a bit."

"I could use a nice cup of tea," I said.

"Not yet," she said. "You've still got some calming down to get used to. Anyway, you really need to eat. You're a little skinny, and we weren't sure it was your natural state. You haven't gotten much to eat besides protein shakes for the last few days. Still, it looks like you're putting on a little weight, anyway."

"Not too much, I hope," I said. I glanced down at my cold, white, skeletal hands. The ink stains were gone for the first time in years.

"Well, now you aren't going to blow away in a stiff breeze."

I lit another cigarette. They tasted awful, but I enjoyed the high. "I'm having some memory issues," I mentioned. "How'd my clothes get here?"

"Your friend Lise brought them, day before yesterday," the doctor replied. "When she found out that you weren't going anywhere for a while. She brought you some clothes and a couple of things—some comics, mostly. They're all safe; they're in a locked box in the ward office."

"So . . ." I said as casually as I could, "I guess she took my journal away, huh?"

"She didn't take it away," she replied simply. "She just didn't bring it. And that was a good piece of mental-health judgment on her part. I don't think it's something you should go back to for a while. She told us all about that. She's been very helpful."

It occurred to me that I had forgotten to say something—"Must hang onto my girlish figure." But now it was too late to say it—if I said it now, it wouldn't make any sense. My thoughts trickled through my brain very slowly. "So . . . writing down my thoughts was pretty much the wrong thing to do?"

"Of course it wasn't."

"It was the only thing keeping me sane."

"But it wasn't you keeping you sane. Nothing was keeping you sane." She gave a charming little laugh that relaxed me despite everything. "And I don't think you should be worrying about what's 'sane' and 'insane' right now. It's not something that's permanent. Don't label yourself. It's just a different state of mind. And there's nothing wrong with being a little dotty. I'm a little dotty myself. The only difference between being charmingly eccentric and being in the inpatient psych ward is how much danger you can be to yourself. And to others."

I grunted, and flicked my cigarette out into a mound of dark brown snow. "Did I hurt anyone?" I asked. "Did I hurt Lise?"

"No, you didn't. You just gave her a good scare. But it was a real scare. And she did the right thing. And so did you; you fought, but you begged for help, and you signed yourself in voluntarily."

"I don't remember doing that," I murmured. "That doesn't . . . sound like something I would do . . ."

Shandy sighed. "Michael, I'd like you to come back inside now with me, and take a look into a mirror. I'm going to see if I can knock some of the last couple of days loose."

I was scared, but I didn't say anything to keep it from happening. I didn't know why I'd be scared.

When I saw myself, though, the nagging, formless fear evaporated. In the small oval glass of a hand mirror, the face I should have recognized looked back at me like a photograph of a war veteran—a black-and-white photograph, at that. My pupils were huge in freakish Keene-painting eyes; both my temples were covered with little cuts, some of them stitched up with blue plastic thread. I had two florid black eyes; there was a purple, clotted, scabby half-moon under my lower lip. "What the fuck?" I whispered, pushing the long hair back out of my face further and taking my glasses off. "Oh. My. Sweet hopping Jesus."

"Those are self-inflicted injuries, Michael. That's where you started trying to keep from being pulled out of the closet by clinging to the door frame with your face." I traced the stitches with my fingertip, and she hissed in sympathetic pain. "Pretty nasty, huh? Gave yourself a nice little concussion there. And when Lise tried to get you out of the apartment, you gracefully flung yourself down the stairs and bit through your lip. That's when she called the ambulance."

I shook my head. "I do not remember that at all," I said, smiling.

"Do you remember that she had to chase you into the custodial closet in the hallway, and then they had to sedate you to get you out?"

I laughed. "No. Wow. Punk rock."

Shandy O'Grady had been somber and straight-faced until this point, when she just gave up and laughed a rich, natural laugh. "Yeah, I guess so. Suicidal tendencies; not just a band anymore. But . . ." She grew serious again. "Lise wasn't very impressed. Mostly she was just terrified."

"I would apologize to her if I could."

"One of these days, you can. What's the earliest thing you remember before you came to the hospital?"

"Being tired," I said, pacing around her office with my hands in my pockets. "I just wanted to keep on sleeping."

"Do your medications make you sleepy?"

"Of course they do," I said. "They make me feel like I'm wrapped in . . . in that kind of fake snow that goes around the base of Christmas trees. That fake snow fluffy cotton shit."

The shrink raised her eyebrows. "That's a great image."

I shrugged. "I answered your question."

"It's called 'flocking,' by the way. I have the feeling that you're going to be just fine, and out of here, oh, in a day or so. Your mother has called every day. She'd like to come get you, if that's all right with you," Shandy said gently.

"I'm not going home with Lise?"

She paused just long enough. "No," she said.

"Can I call her?"

Shandy looked pained. "No. She specifically asked that you didn't. I'm sure she must need some time on her own to examine her feelings. And to give you some time for you to think, too."

I swallowed. "Did I hurt her?"

"Some bruises, that's all. You struggled; that's all. But you were also begging for her to help you. She knows you didn't mean to hurt her. Mostly I think she just wants to know you're all right."

My hands ached. "Can I have a pen and some paper?" I asked.

"I don't think you're really ready for that yet, Michael."

"Please. Call me Squire," I said.

I got up after a good twelve hours' sleep, put on the clean flannel shirt and blue jeans that I pulled out of the duffel bag next to my bed, and went to breakfast with the other lunatics. The other inpatients really didn't seem all that bad, actually—some of them were going through drug withdrawal, and a couple of them, like Lewis, were actually a little bit cracked, but mostly they just seemed a little tired out and jumpy. There was one very fat woman who yelled triumphantly every time the commercials stopped and the game show came back on, and pretended she knew all the answers to all the questions. I saw people crazier than her on the bus every day.

The orderly who was always guiding me around led me to Shandy O'Grady's office after breakfast, and opened the door for me. "You like Shandy?" he asked me.

"She's cool," I shrugged

"She's pretty cute, ain't she?"

"Sort of," I said. "Not really my type. Her butt's not big enough."

"I like the way you think, Mike." He gave me a solid, manly trick handshake.

Shandy was working at her desk when I went in. She looked a little frazzled; her hair was up in one big messy ponytail with big straggles going down into her face. I sat down in the overstuffed chair opposite her, feeling somewhat superior; I looked like a sane, normal kid, and she looked like an addled hysteric. "I'll be with you in just a minute," she said, going back to her scribbling and shuffling of paper. "Tons of paperwork all of a sudden."

"Take your time," I said, smiling.

She looked up. She smiled and folded her hands on her desk. "Okay, you win," she said.

"No, I was serious."

"How are you today?"

"Full of butter," I said. "And protein shake."

"How's your head feel?"

"Mostly in one piece," I said, touching the stitches. "Still kind of hurts. At least it hurts now—I couldn't really feel it before."

"You ready to go home and stay with your mother for a while? Take it easy?" she asked.

"Uh . . . I guess so?" I said.

"You're going to be discharged tomorrow," said Shandy. "I'd suggest that you go with her. Your apartment on Belmont isn't going to be where you live from now on."

"No?"

"Your girlfriend—Lise Ballard was your girlfriend, right?"

"*Was*? What, is she dead?"

"No, no; she's fine. She moved out of that place. She's gone to meet her father in Indonesia, and then they're going to Australia. She's going to help him out with his documentaries."

"Oh . . . that's cool, I guess," I murmured.

"How do you feel about that?"

I shrugged. "I dunno, how am I supposed to feel? I think it's cool. She always did want to be closer to her dad. Shooting nature documentaries is on the cool side. And she's away from that blasted, satanic copy shop. Never thought she'd leave that fucking place."

Shandy paused in boring a hole through her desk calendar with a pen. "Were you jealous of her job?"

"No. I don't know." I shrugged again. "It's moot now. Moot."

"That's your call," said Shandy. "Back to the matter at hand; do you want to see your mother?"

"I said yeah, didn't I? Do I have a choice?"

"Do you want a choice?"

"Choice is good," I said. "I like to think I'm not a prisoner being transferred between cell blocks. 'Shut down all the garbage compactors on Level AA23'—you know what that's from?"

She didn't blink. "*Star Wars.* I'm a doctor, not an idiot. You'll have to try a little harder than that if you're trying to challenge me."

"Point," I said, chuckling.

Shandy slid the telephone on her desk towards me. "Call your mother," she said calmly. "Tell her to come get you. Tomorrow, at two."

I stared at Shandy. "Uh . . ." I hadn't spoken on the phone in months, and truth be told, I'd forgotten Mom's number.

"Go on," said Shandy. "You can handle this. I've talked to Marion. She's an all-right lady. And she promised me she wouldn't hassle you. Here's the number—she's staying at a bed-and-breakfast in Northwest."

"But—I—"

"It's just a telephone call. There's nobody on the other end except your mom. This extension goes right to her room. And if she's not there, leave her a message. You can do it."

I picked up the receiver, and before I could hear a dial tone, punched in the number, scribbled on a pink Post-It in blue highlighter.

She answered in a tired, distracted voice. "This is Marion Fortensky," she said.

My heart shattered as if it had been dipped in liquid nitrogen. "Mom?"

"Hi, sweetheart," she said again, her voice suddenly warm and personable. It bubbled slightly with restrained laughter, and she sighed happily. "How ya doin'?"

"Okay. Better," I said.

"Good," she said. "Mind a visitor?"

"Not as long as you get me out of here," I said.

"No problem. I'll be there tomorrow afternoon. We'll go grab a bite to eat, and then we'll drive back home. Should be pretty—it's pretty snowy, you know."

"It is?" I asked.

"It is. It snowed last night. Still coming down a little bit. It's nice."

I sat there and listened to the not-silence on the line. It sounded like distilled nothing, as though none of us was connected to anything. My face felt very hot, then wet. "I'm sorry, Mom."

"What for, baby? You didn't do anything wrong."

"Who's paying for this hospital stay? It can't be cheap."

"None of your business who's paying. It'll be paid for. I just want you to relax for a while—for as long as you need to. It's all okay. Everything's fine now." Her voice drifted off into a lazy, quiet lilt, the soft tone of voice she used to use on me when I was hurt or sick and having problems getting to sleep. My mother never sang to me, only spoke in her half-whisper, usually reading something like Tim Leary's *Psychedelic Prayer*. "Okay? I'll see you tomorrow. Take care. I love you, honey."

"Okay, bye," I said, and hung up.

Shandy was smiling at me. "See, that was easy," she said.

"For you, maybe," I said. I wiped my face. The salt stung the cut beneath my lip.

"You're just having feelings. You're doing fine."

"I *am* heavily medicated," I added.

We laughed.

"Do you feel better?"

"Kind of," I admitted. "I wish I could talk to Lise, though. I want to apologize to her."

"There'll be time for that. But right now, she has to do what she needs to do for herself. You have to go live your life every day, and not spend too much time thinking about the reasons why. I'm no psychoanalyst. If you're interested in psychoanalysis, go for it, but I'm not your gal. I'm a psychiatric nurse practitioner. I don't think that knowing the reasons why we feel the way we do gives us any kind of upper hand on dealing with those emotions, those moods, when they come. We just have feelings. Every one of us does." She sipped out of a chipped mug that had obviously been handmade by a child, glazed sloppily in bright green with a big shamrock painted on the side in darker green. "You can, however, take past experiences and put them to good use. You're a creative person. That might work to your advantage. You can't forget these experiences, but you don't have to let them control you. You can control them."

"I don't know if I buy that creative stuff," I said. "Never did me any good before. Is—is that coffee?"

"Yes."

"Real coffee? Like, with caffeine?"

She squinted at me. "I've never seen eyes twinkle like that in real life. Like, little coffee cups with hearts appeared in your eyes. No, you can't have any. Anyway, I have a cold."

"Aw, crap."

"Squire, concentrate. We really don't have very much time. What kinds of things will make you happy about going home to stay with your mother for a while? You do like your mother, don't you? You sound like you get along pretty well."

"Yeah, I love my mom . . . She's one of my best friends, actually. There's a lot of good things about living at home. I can read whatever books I want, and I have my own art room, and my mother's friends are . . . pretty cool, sometimes." I meant that they gave me free drugs, but I didn't think it was appropriate to mention that. "All kinds of stuff."

"And what will you miss about living on your own?"

". . . I was with Lise." Sex. Being able to roll over in bed and feel those yards of soft, supple, funky-smelling skin, being able to lick the pheromones directly from her moist armpits, teasing her wet lower lips with the head of my prick. I remembered all these things with a shock of loss.

"What kinds of things will you miss about living with Lise?"

"What—what—what difference does it make?" My face was hot.

"I'd like you to start thinking about it now, when you're in a position to get help about the way you feel, rather than later, when you might not have that luxury."

"What difference does it make if I get 'help'?" I quirked my fingers in the air.

Shandy sat back in her chair and regarded me calmly. "What do you need from me to feel safe?"

"Safe from what?"

"You tell me."

"I thought you weren't a psychotherapist," I muttered.

"Do you want me to stop asking questions? All right, I will. Ask yourself the questions. I want you to start thinking about what kinds of things you want, and don't want, and what you can stand, and what you can't. And try some new things. You might be surprised at how easy they are. Like, when was the last time you calmly picked up the telephone and called someone? And talked to them? Do you actually remember?"

"No," I said.

"See? And I have the feeling you spent a long time thinking that something like that was impossible. It doesn't matter what methods you use to make yourself feel secure and safe—you can tell yourself you're Superman, if it makes a difference."

I snickered.

"What?"

"Superman sucks," I said.

Shandy shrugged. "Okay, who's a superhero you can stand? Who's got some qualities that you can appreciate? And don't dare say Batman—he's a pathological case."

"All superheroes are," I said. "Every superhero has something seriously wrong with them. If they had superpowers and perfect lives, they'd be totally boring."

"Exactly. What's one you identify with?"

I shrugged. "Well, Batman, pretty much," I mumbled guiltily. Shandy grinned and rolled her eyes. "Maybe one of the X-Men. Nightcrawler. Or Freakshow. I've always considered myself something of a mutant."

"That much is obvious." She glanced at her wall clock. "I have to see another patient now. What are you going to do?"

"Go back to the common room and see if I can score a crossword puzzle or something," I said. "Sometimes the Igors forget to steal it out of the paper."

"'Igors'? That's a new way of thinking about it. Lemme see—I have today's paper, and I'm done with it," Shandy said. "You want any more of it?"

"Just the crossword. I have enough neurosis inside me without having to look at the world's problems."

"Very astute." She tore out the page with the crossword and the comics and the TV schedule on it. "I'm afraid you'll have to get a pencil from the nurses' station. And expect them to watch you like a hawk so that you don't do anything, you know, crazy."

I saluted her. "Scout's honor, ma'am."

"Oh, bullshit. See you tomorrow. You're doing great. Let DeShawn or Annette know if you need anything today." She smiled and shook her head, returning to the pile of paperwork on her desk. I gave her a little wave as soon as I thought she couldn't see me.

The next morning I went to Shandy's office again. I had looked forward to it since yesterday. She had her hair down; it was very long and I saw that the red was a very artificial color with dull blonde roots. She wore a black cardigan over a white t-shirt and grey jeans and no makeup at all. "Hi, Squire," she said.

"You look pretty," I said.

"Really? Thanks."

"Do you get patients falling in love with you all the time?"

"Usually not—I've been doing inpatient assessment for most of my career, which means I don't see very many patients more than once. If they're going to be around for a long time, they end up going to the state hospital or a group home—we don't have facilities for more than twenty patients at a time. You get to go home very soon, which is great, and I am very impressed. You turned in a relatively lucid and honest questionnaire yesterday, and I can literally see the improvement in you. You have good 'affect', as we call it."

"It's probably because I used conditioner on my hair today," I said. "It has body, shine, and good affect."

"Very funny. I bet you're itchin' to get out of here, huh? Your mom will be here in a little while; I'd like to talk to both of you together for a while, then her by herself, while you're getting your stuff together. Is that going to be okay?"

"Sure it is. If I don't get away from *Joker's Wild* reruns, I really will end up in the loony bin."

Shandy smiled. "You are in the loony bin," she reminded me.

"I'm talking about the long-term loony bin."

"There is a big difference," she nodded, blowing her nose on a pink tissue. "For example, it's pretty easy to get out of here. It's hard to get out of there. And, Squire, I hope you don't take this the wrong way, but I really hope I don't hear about you being in there. It is possible to do something about your issues—I'm not one of those psychiatrists who thinks that every kind of emotional disturbance is caused by an imbalance of chemicals. I believe you have some measure of control over what you do when people are shitty to you—and they often are. Other people are assholes, but they have their own problems to deal with, and sometimes they say and do things that are hurtful, but not out of malice. In your case, I really think you are able to strike some kind of balance between thinking you're God, and thinking you're Satan. You're just a person. You have thoughts, and feelings, and impulses that other people just don't understand. And that's okay."

I had the tremendous urge to pick my nose. Instead I shrugged and looked out the window. "Yeah, I know," I acknowledged.

"Just think, you can have coffee in about two hours!" Shandy said. She reached behind her desk and rifled around in her Guatemalan hippie purse. "I made you a mix tape," she added, sliding it across the desk calendar at me. "I hope you don't mind."

"What is it, subliminal self-esteem stuff?"

"No, it's just plain music. It's got some Pixies, and some Eurythmics; a new Björk track, some Echo and the Bunnymen—"

"Bunnymen?" My voice was a broken, desperate whisper.

She smiled a beautiful smile. "I love Echo and the Bunnymen. They were my favorite band when I was in high school."

"Can I be trusted with that?" I was kidding, but not.

"It's just music, Squire," Shandy said. "It's just one track."

"Which one?"

"'Ocean Rain.' It's soothing."

"Oh." Yeah. That was safe. I actually sang softly, to myself, "I'm at sea again, now my hurricane has brought down this ocean rain to bathe me again. . ." I just sang. I didn't care. Shandy smiled, calm and kind, neither impressed nor repulsed. I had never sung aloud in front of someone in my life, and it was all right.

"Music is good," she said. "I know how important it is to you."

"Thank you," I said. She gave a single nod. "No, really. I don't have anything anymore. I sold it all." I rolled my eyes, groaning at the memory, but she didn't seem fazed by that statement.

"You were manic," she explained. "I'm sure it seemed like a good idea at the time. Now you can listen to the tape, and write back to me, and tell me which ones you like. Might give you some ideas about rebuilding your collection."

The tape case had a magazine clipping of an unhappy-wet-diaper-baby advertisement. I loved it. I asked, "So who's your favorite band?"

She smiled. "Pussy Galore. I also really like Mr. Bungle."

I gaped. "Where did you *come* from?"

"I'm just a white suburban punk," she replied calmly, "just like you."

A knock came at the door before I could leap over the desk and start kissing Shandy passionately. It was DeShawn, which went a long way towards helping put my heart back in my chest and my libido back in my jeans. Shandy called for him to come in; the orderly poked his head in and smiled at us. "Mrs. Fortensky is here," he said.

"It's Ms.," I corrected compulsively.

168

"Let it go, Squire," Shandy said softly. "So," she said, her voice louder and firmer, "are you ready?"

We went to the main social room, which was empty except for DeShawn and my mother. She turned and spotted me. "Hi," she announced. I stopped short at the sight of her, so unchanged—my usual typical Mom, wearing an Army-surplus parka and a dark-brown corduroy jumper and hiking boots. Her hair was frizzy and her eyeglasses were smudged. She looked amazing. And she just smiled at me like I'd won a prize. And yet at the same time I didn't feel anything. It didn't seem real. Maybe I had just dreamt the whole thing.

She came in, and shook Shandy's hand. "Hi. Marion."

"Shandy."

"Very nice to meet you." Mom turned to me at last, and hugged me very quickly and kissed the top of my head.

"You doing okay, baby?" she asked.

"Yeah," I said.

I was discharged after a ton of paperwork, bearing a grocery sack rattling with pill bottles. Mom and I walked with great purpose towards the nearest CoffeeFolks, which was less than two blocks from the hospital. It was bitter cold and damp outside—perfect coffee weather. The snow had become gray slush.

"Coffee, coffee, coffee, hooray. Oh, yeah! I almost forgot—I brought you your Christmas presents," Mom said, poking me in the shoulder.

"Cool!"

"I have your stuff from the apartment in my car."

"Yeah . . . okay." Oh, God. My life. It was gone. Not *over*, though, which was even more surreal.

"Do you have any cash?" Mom asked.

"Not on me." I had no idea how much I might have in the bank.

"Okay, I'll buy you coffee."

I almost burnt my tongue on the hot coffee, I was so eager to drink it, and blew the warm sweet steam in a cloud around my face. Mom sat down by the window and cautiously stirred her own drink. "Honey, don't take this the wrong way, but you look like shit. How do you feel?"

"Hungry."

"You got a headache, or anything?"

I shook my head. "I just need the coffee," I said. "And can we go to Taco Bell?"

Mom grimaced. "If that's what you want. *I* think it's gross, but . . ."

"Craving, Mom; wicked craving."

In the car, the stereo played Jeff Buckley. She lit cigarettes for both of us. I brushed Taco Bell shredded cheese food off the new, crisp gray wool trousers she'd brought me, and accepted the cigarette. "When did you start smoking again?" I asked.

"When I got on the internet," she said. "It was just so stressful."

"I heard that," I said.

The road was slick with icy rain and a deep, bluish fog hung over the farmlands, the sapling farms, the billboards that read "Jesus Christ Died For Your Sins." Mom sang along with the doomed younger Buckley, hitting the crazy high notes so accurately that she must have sung along to it hundreds of times. I knew she was into the father, Tim Buckley, and had actually met the man, but she'd gotten into Jeff's music while I was busy looking the other way. Jeff Buckley had died earlier that year, in May, and I had never bothered to listen to his music. And now he was dead, and my mom had memorized every note of "Grace."

Mom and her dead guys. I wasn't going to judge. It was a really good song.

On the drive I kept waiting for an overwhelming sense of relief to pour over me, but nothing came—nothing whatsoever. I was a blank slate—or more accurately, a perfect sheet of diamond. I contained nothing, and nothing could make an impression on my surface. I was out there in the fog, with the wooden slats of the signs, with the blades of grass, nodding heavily with droplets of ice. Still waiting to find . . . something.

The first thing I did when I got to Bellingham, besides taking a shit, taking a twenty-minute nap, and staring into the fridge for a while, was to get a new pair of glasses. My trusty black vintage Army-issue frames were a wreck of scratch-fogged lenses and earpieces mended with layers of tape, and my eye prescription had changed, somewhat for the better. Against my mother's hopes (she favored that Lennon-esque schoolboy wire-rim thing), I got more black plastic frames, these rectangular and vaguely suggesting half-glasses for reading. "Now you look at least eighteen," said the girl at Binyon's. She was smiling all over me and twirling her hair around her forefinger. I told her that trichotillomania, the nervous worrying of one's own hair, was an obsessive-compulsive disorder, and had she considered twenty-five milligrams of Anafranil a day? I tapped a couple out into my palm to show her, and she shivered and went to the back room. "Way to let her know that you're not interested," my mother quipped, waiting for her credit card transaction to go through. "It might have been simpler just to tell her you're gay."

I had no idea what she was talking about for over an hour.

The second thing I did was to listen to Shandy's tape. I sat in my childhood bedroom, which was now a sewing/storage/book/guest room, eating slices of bread and brie. It was a great tape, really expertly done. I immediately began thinking of tracks to make a mix in return. I had the address of the hospital on the prescription labels of my various bottles of pills.

At eleven o'clock, my mother sat and watched me take Ativan, Zyprexa, and Lamictal, and watched me get in bed. "Love you, kid," she said.

"Thank you, Mom," I said. Through force of will, I did not weep from gratitude, even though it made my eyes hurt to hold back the tears. I didn't want her to worry.

After a few weeks of slacking, sitting around the house watching cartoons and children's television, taking walks by myself, and tidying up the apartment, my mother decided that I should work with her in the bookstore. She'd just had to fire some flaky chick who came to work drunk and would berate any man unlucky enough to pass over the threshold. "You're the perfect employee in a feminist/new age bookstore," Mom said. "There's not a woman alive who could possibly be intimidated by you." I took it as the compliment she intended.

I do the shelving, the receiving, the cash drawer, the vacuuming of Bing-Bing's hairs off the flat industrial carpet, the wiping of the big glass window that looks out onto the lonesome street by the train tracks, and this summer, I repainted the signs and the façade. No hurry, no pressure.

I found many more pictures of my father than I remembered existed, books and books of them, his fingerprints, his incredibly clumsy watercolors, and his fractured, shattered, beautiful poetry. I don't know if they were individual poems or just stanzas grouped on the page—I read them as one large piece, and as individual poems. They gave me the creeps—stuff like

> A SINGLE CURL
>
> SNIPPED FROM THE LIFE
>
> OF A LITTLE GIRL

and

> AMARANTH PASSED ON TODAY
>
> AUNTIE WORRIES NOT
>
> SHE'S GOT THE LEASE
>
> TO HER FLAT IN SOUTH KENSINGTON
>
> (31 JAN 68)

In February I cut my hair short, started wearing fuzzy tweed jackets, pleated cotton slacks in muted colors, argyle socks, polished cordovan oxfords, sweater vests—in other words, I bought a bunch of new clothes at the Goodwill that made me look like a sixty-year-old professor. The teenage town girls go wild for a man with corduroy patches on his elbows. No, seriously, they do. I maintain my aloofness, and they just see it as a challenge. I'm getting a bit spoiled by the attention, and I also don't know what to do with it.

I started painting again. It's not any good, but it's something to do.

This spring, as well, my mother stopped leaving me to my own devices and insisted that I get out as much as possible. That's how I met Larry. There was a morning when I just didn't really want to be at work. It was a completely dead day, the first sunny day of spring this year, and people were either trapped at work or they were out hiking. My mother was busy decorating frantically for something and I sat on the counter, cleaning my ear with a Q-Tip. She turned around and went completely bonkers, yelling incoherently at me. "What? What did I do?" I begged.

"Feet off the counter—and stop scraping your brains with that Q-Tip. Get out of here. You're driving me crazy with that nonsense. Go have breakfast somewhere—I know you didn't eat, I heard you banging around on that balcony this morning. Out out out."

I grabbed an issue of *Scientific American*, and crossed the tracks to Angelique's. I sat at the bar. Again, there was nobody there, and Pilar, the manageress, practically breathed down my neck until I ordered something. I got steak and eggs, and coffee in the mug I left in the café.

"What's that, steak and eggs?" asked a man who was suddenly sitting next to me at the bar.

I nodded with my mouth full, keeping the magazine cracked to the story I was in the middle of reading. The guy was about my mother's age, hair gray and thinning, thick glasses and a face like a mile of bad road. "I'll have what he's having," he shouted to Pilar.

"Okay, Larry," she shouted back, sounding sick of him already.

The man gave an impatient sigh that took years off him—there was something of adolescent boredom in that one little sigh. He explained to me, "She has never liked me, and I've been so nice to her all this time." He looked over my shoulder again. "*SciAm?*"

"Yeah," I said. "Bruce Sterling article in it."

"Bruce is okay, but you really have to read folks like Stainslaw Lem, or, or, like Heinlein. Young people think Heinlein is a cliché, but that's because the man is an astonishing talent."

"I've never read Heinlein seriously, so I can't really offer any insights into why the young people have such an idea." Yes, I was being sarcastic, trying to get rid of him, but he didn't let me off so easily.

He offered his hand. "Lawrence Trevino Suttman," he said, "but call me Larry."

"Squire." I shook the hand, as scaly and heavy as a glove made of rhinoceros hide. His grip was brief, but I could tell that he could smash my bones to marmalade if he wanted to. "Are you trying to pick me up?"

"By talking about Heinlein? Wow, you *are* an erudite man, aren't you?" I expected him to call me a "little" something, but not just "man." It was unsettling. I was *kid*, I was *boy*, I was *Poindexter*, I wasn't *man*. But I could be, I guess. "Heavens, no. I'm a heterosexual. Anyway, you're far too young, even if I weren't. Tell me, do you stargaze?"

"Like, watching constellations and planets and stuff? Sure, a little bit."

"It isn't just watching constellations and planets and stuff. It's looking into space—the history of our galaxy, including the past and the future. Astrology isn't all just bullshit, pal. It's mostly bullshit, of course—

but there's more information out there than most people even care to find."

"I have a telescope," I said. "It's not in focus."

"I have several telescopes. Some of them are excellent. I could probably get yours into decent shape, if you'd like."

"Might I ask why you're asking me about all this?" I asked.

Pilar slammed his plate of steak and eggs down in front of him. Larry looked up and thanked her with a huge smile. "Hm?" he started, returning to me. "Oh, well . . . you're the only other one here."

After breakfast we went to my house to get the telescope. Larry went into the bookstore and stood there with his hands jammed into the pockets of his threadbare wool overcoat. I went straight in and my mother asked, "Who is that?"

"That's Larry Sutton," I said. "He says he can focus my telescope."

"Oh, I bet he can," said Mom.

Larry smiled, and thrust forth his hand. "Larry," he said.

"Marion," she replied. "That's my son, Squire."

"Yes, I know. I met him at Angelique's. I think he's a fascinating person—alive with potential."

"Potential to be what?" My mother crossed her arms.

"Well—well, anything, really. He could be anything at all." He smiled at her. "And no, I'm not trying to pick him up, but I won't make any promises about you."

"Oh, *that's* tasteful. Thank you, I'm flattered and disgusted, all at the same time. Squire, get out of here, okay? See how the actual crazies of the town are, and see how much better you are in comparison."

I went upstairs and got my telescope, and when I got back, he and my mother were still quipping at each other, having gotten the attention of everyone else in the store. "You, of all people, should be more generous about recognizing human potential," Larry was shaking his head.

"There's a difference between recognizing potential and encouraging people's silliness—oh, Squire, please rescue me from Mr. Transcendentalism here before I develop the human potential give him a solid, uncompromising knuckle sandwich. Do me a favor and be back here by two in the morning—I don't expect you any earlier."

I went over to her and kissed her. "I've got my meds with me," I whispered in her ear. "Don't worry." She rolled her eyes.

And I went over to his house, a little ways outside of town on the edge of a hill that was clearcut in the seventies and grew back with small trees and crab grass. The house was full of things—glass containers, large-format artwork, Christmas decorations, and thousands of books. He sat me down in an incredibly comfortable chair, made me a hot toddy, and stuck a big color book of Galileo's research into my hands. "Read that," he said. "I'm going to get cracking on that telescope."

We ended up stargazing that night, on a Gore-Tex blanket on that hill, drinking hot chocolate with whiskey out of a Thermos, and watching the Magic Marker white swish of the full moon as it crested the forest canopy. The sky was more beautiful than anytime I'd ever seen it, gorged full of stars and flocked with pearly pink clouds. "Wow! I forgot about the sky!" I shouted into the solid quiet. "It's so—it's so—"

"Isn't it wonderful? It's the best and the worst part of being alive. You know the meteors are going to come from there, but it's sure gonna be beautiful."

"Is it okay if I yell a lot for a while?" I asked.

"Sure!"

We yelled for a good long time until we couldn't breathe for laughing. I felt quite drained afterward, as if I'd just gotten rid of the parts of myself that I didn't need. He whistled softly and said, "Goddamn. Sometimes it's worth it, isn't it?"

He told me all about himself—how he'd been in Vietnam as a clerk or something and never saw any combat, only the aftermath; came back and got married and had two kids, then one day woke up in a screaming panic that wouldn't let up for six months. Trying to lead a normal life was just a little too much for him. He was sent to the state hospital in Olympia for two years, where he was given electroconvulsive shock to cure his depression. While he was in, his wife left him for a real estate developer and moved to Fort Lauderdale. He keeps in very close contact with his teenaged kids, who ran away with an international tumbler's circus and travel all over the world.

I told him all about Portland, and Lise, and the hospital, and the chilling expression of the man in the bed beside me as he looked at the full moon. "There you go," Larry said. "That was saying something. Some people are able to pay attention to it. Ever get those sensations of greatness, a sort of tremendous crushing greatness? That's the universe talking to you. Listen to it. And don't think that because that happens to you, that you're the center of the universe. You are not."

"Well, I know that now," I replied, a little confused and annoyed.

"And that's not what I'm getting at either, man. I'm not saying you did anything wrong. You weren't wrong, and you weren't crazy. Those drugs they've got you on—that's good—the compulsions you were having, the tendency to strip all things down to a few essentials, that was a good step, but you have to get beyond that. Psychoactive drugs help you to come down into yourself, figure out what you really want. You're in the process of figuring out. Myself, I know more or less what I want—I want to avoid apocalypse. That's all I want. And I'll sit here and try out strategies until I figure out how to do it."

"Apocalypse?" I whispered, the word too powerful to say out loud.

He took a big swig from the Thermos. "From above," he said. "You're not crazy."

And that started it. We've touched base with each other every day since then.

He's a real American hybrid, from Tacoma or something, who did his share of acid and biker chicks in the Sixties and has the ravaged skin to prove it. Now he's quieter, always a little hunched over; he wears ratty dress pants and a white shirt and tie, always the tie. Sometimes he goes weeks forgetting to shave, and then appears well-brushed and smooth and shiny with his pants pressed like an FBI agent's, often bringing my mother a freshly picked flower or a random pretty object, like a piece of broken safety glass or a little rubber dinosaur. Mom says he looks like a repo man, and I have to admit, he's got that kind of washed-out, ex-bookie look about him. Kids at the elementary school run away when he walks past their schoolyard because they think he's creepy. He gives a great Haunted House every Halloween that scares the piss out of the little brats and gives them nightmares that last for weeks.

I asked my mother once why she disliked him so much. "Oh, well, I don't so much dislike him as . . ." She hemmed and hawed. "Okay, I dislike him."

"But why? He's nuts about you."

"That's exactly what gives me the creeps."

"Really? Do you think he's crazy?" I asked casually.

"Yes, I do," she sighed. "And I don't know how I feel about you hanging out with him."

"Insanity isn't actually contagious," I said, walking out the door, heading off to meet him for another round of whiskeys at the Salamander. "You can't get it by touching someone."

Of course, this was nonsense—anyone who's been there knows full well that insanity is contagious. It spreads through groups of people like a virus, and some people have a natural resistance to it and they don't catch it. Some people breathe in the atmosphere and, shortly, they're on the other side of the mirror. And some of us catch it, suffer from it, and forge an immunity. There's a reason why so many schizophrenics and neurotics work in the mental health field—they're like parents who've had chicken pox, being able to nurse their stricken children.

We recognize each other.

Larry is a prolific diarist himself, in the form, mostly, of lab notes and astronomical observations. I've sat and read his journals like books—lists of inclinations and degrees, newspaper clippings of unexplained phenomena, "Tues. nite—drank .5 litres of neat grain alcohol and ingested 3 g. *amanita muscaria* on empty stomach. Bouts of vomiting and communication with beings who live in the Crab Nebula. They promise positive reinforcements P.A." *P.A.* was a common abbreviation—post apocalypse. I don't think he's on to something, but he might be on to something.

I had forgotten what it was like to have a friend. Just a friend. I think he needed me.

I'm done reading the journals. I'm fresh out. Kind of too bad—I always did enjoy my bit of solipsism, the same as most any writer. One's own writing has a peculiar smell, a particular liquid flow of being read that makes you just breeze through the pages, like you're reading someone else's mind. In my case, it really feels like someone else's mind. I don't remember a lot of the states I was in when I was writing that stuff down. Where was I at this time last year?

I don't keep a journal anymore. I haven't since Before. I just live through life without documenting it. There is nobody to corroborate my story, to help me prove to myself, or anyone else, that any of it happened. That doesn't really bother me, actually—I never have to prove that any of it was real, all I have to do is state it. I don't really care if the things I wrote about ever actually happened that way—as far as that tiny lettering on that Eye-Eaze yellowish paper goes, it happened.

Now that I have the journals back, and I've had a chance to read them over completely, I can use them as the basis for my greatest creative work—and it isn't even fiction. All of it is true.

Well, sure, *some* of it was delusion.

THE MIXTAPE TRACKLIST

Björk - Joga
Echo and the Bunnymen - All In My Mind
Messiah - Temple of Dreams
Gern Blanston - Headbag
TMBG - Where Your Eyes Don't Go
Brian Eno - Discreet Music
Echo and the Bunnymen - The Back of Love
Echo and the Bunnymen - Rescue
Echo and the Bunnymen- Stars are Stars
Snoopy Come Home Official Soundtrack - It Changes
Echo and the Bunnymen - Over the Wall
Echo and the Bunnymen - Seven Seas
Creedence Clearwater Revival - Proud Mary
Grateful Dead - Magnolia Rose
Echo and the Bunnymen - Villiers Terrace
Spinner - Where We Lived
The Smiths - There is a Light that Never Goes Out
Ian McCulloch - Magical World
Duran Duran - Sound of Thunder
Echo and the Bunnymen - The Yo-Yo Man
The Rolling Stones - Paint It Black
Echo and the Bunnymen - Going Up
The Doors - The End
Echo and the Bunnymen - Nocturnal Me
Echo and the Bunnymen - Blue Blue Ocean
Jacqueline Du Pré - Haydn: Cello Concerto #1 in D
Jeff Buckley - Grace
Eurythmics - Doubleplusgood

Jemiah Jefferson was born in Denver, Colorado in 1972. Her publications include the Vampire Quartet novels *Voice of the Blood*, *Wounds*, *Fiend*, and *A Drop of Scarlet*, and the legendary erotic short-story chapbook *ST*RF*CK*NG*. An avid fan of great music, bad movies, sci-fi television, and comics, she lives in Portland, Oregon.

Made in the USA
Lexington, KY
08 February 2014